T0067563

THE
LESSER-KNOWN
GHARDAVIAN
TALES

for Mummy and Daddy, who are an
eternal source of inspiration,

for Amiji and Abuji, who set a great example
for me to start everything from scratch

PREFACE

It was on a very cold evening last year in the month of December, while narrating a story to my youngest cousin Aayan, a very simple thought struck my mind – 'Why don't I write my own stories?' As a child I had never really taken keen interest in literature or English as a language but the thought of writing my own stories was so exhilarating that I was ready to start everything from a scratch. I had not been well versed with the language, neither did I have enough practice but that is the beauty of life – we all have to start at some point.

The credit for the trillions of stories that reside in my brain goes solely to my mother. As growing up she would always take out time from her hectic schedule and narrate bedtime stories to my brothers and me. Instead of us falling asleep, my mother would be the one whom we would find fast asleep. I still remember how we would nudge her and force her to complete the stories. I will never forget those times when everything seemed so magical, well actually, everything still is.

For me writing has been an ongoing battle but maybe that is how it is supposed to be. Staring at that blank sheet of paper can be very haunting but when you face your fears and overcome them, you get your reward and that reward is the 'voice' your thoughts get. I have learnt a lot from this simple yet complicated project I undertook last year.

I initially began writing this collection of stories and poems in hope to raise money for the 2014 Kashmir floods and as time passed the reasons for me to continue writing grew stronger. There were just so many things I could accomplish through this simple skill that I was determined to face my vulnerability and continue penning my thoughts down. There are so many people who need help, so many people whose voices are left unheard. I am just preparing myself to be a voice for all those voiceless beings.

Most of us fear taking risks and we dread stepping out of our comfort zones. Truth be told, even I was scared of taking risks and would often try staying on the safe side but this book is my certificate of progress. Completing the book in the midst of the most crucial year of any school student's life was perhaps the risk that had once scared me but I did it anyway and I have no regrets.

Now, I may sound like a sage but I feel it my duty to let all my readers know that I am still a novice. I still struggle to write and I still feel vulnerable when I am not able to think. The point I intend to draw across is that this book is only a whisper, for my true voice is yet to follow. Just like a baby first learns to babble, I am babbling too. Just like a child then learns to talk, I will talk too. There are a million miles to go and I am proud to say that I have given my journey a great start!

Sheik Safwan Fayaz
December 2014

Srinagar, Kashmir

The Enchanted Phirran

For Dania,
whose red Phirran inspired me to write this one

PRE - REQUISITE KNOWLEDGE -

A Phirran is a long cloak-like clothing that is worn in Kashmir. It is a traditional dress and is worn by men and women alike; however, the Phirran made for women is much fancier than the one made for males.

Glossary

Jaana - A term of endearment
Ammai – 'Mother' in Kashmiri language
Abbai – 'Father' in Kashmiri language
Dastar- Khwan – A Persian word which means a large dining spread
Jigar – Loved one
Jaan – Dear
Allah-ki-kasam – To swear to God
Kabristan – A graveyard
Myano Khudaiyo – Oh my God!
Wadun ma hya – Don't Cry
Fajr – The Morning Prayer

CHAPTER 1

The sun was ready to set, to hide behind the mighty mountains of the Kashmir valley. The whole of Srinagar was filled with the joyous chirps of the thousands of birds who were now returning to their homes, to their Chinar trees. It sure had been a long day.

As Latifa watched the sunset, the smile on her face faded away. Another day had gone by and she had yet again not been able to find any medicines for her ailing mother. She only wondered as to what would happen next.

The street was covered in mud and was adorned with various puddles that spread along its path. Latifa held on to her red scarf with one hand and used the other to clutch her long Phirran tight and began hopping her way to her home, crossing one puddle after the other. Every time she made an attempt to hop over the puddles, her curvy eyebrows would rise and she would purse her strawberry lips. Her eyes slowly lost their colour, for she too was losing hope. 'Would her mother ever be able to fight her illness?' Latifa wondered.

The floods had destroyed everything. The smallest of the food reserves had now finished. Latifa's own house was under water for weeks till the water finally dried out, however, leaving behind a complete mess. All the streets and the houses were left covered in thick layers of mud and no one could ever forget the pungent smell that came in as a complementary dish.

As Latifa made her way through the barren street, she took a sharp right and followed the bricked path till she stopped in front of a small red coloured iron gate. She stared at the rusted knob for a while as thousands of thoughts mingled inside her head. She closed her eyes and took a deep breath. She couldn't face it. She couldn't fake sleeping one more night, ignoring the misery her mother was facing due to the illness. In the deepest of her consciousness she knew the reality even when her father would try to edge her away from the truth.

'Everything will be alright,' she whispered to herself in Kashmiri as she very slowly made her way to the main door of the house. The door creaked as Latifa stepped inside her house. The stale air inside the house made it difficult for Latifa to breathe, and the mud (that had yet not been cleared from the floor) dirtied her shoes. The pace of events is so slow here, in this mighty Kashmir of ours. She climbed the first set of stairs and had barely reached the entrance of the Kitchen-cum-room when she heard someone shout in outrage. Her grandmother was cursing Zaida for what Latifa guessed was her 'very careless behavior'.

Zaida was the housemaid whom Latifa's grandmother described as 'utter nuisance in this world'. A 14-year-old beauty was she when she had been brought to Latifa's household. Latifa, on the other hand, had barely been a year old. Zaida, it seemed, was Latifa's foster mother even when Latifa's real mother was still alive and there never was a time in Latifa's life when Zaida was not around to guide her and help her.

As Latifa entered, she noticed her father sitting in one corner of the room. All faces shot up but no one uttered a word. It was Zaida who finally broke the awkward silence.

'Did you find any...' She began when Latifa's grandmother shushed her.

Latifa heaved a sigh, tightened her scarf and looked down on the floor.

'All the shutters were down. Everything was closed,' she said, looking up at her father who was still sitting the same way.

'Abbai, we must go. We must leave now or *Amai* won't make it. She will di...' Latifa trembled. Her eyes grew red and welled up with tears.

'Abbai?'

Her father shot a red eye at her and Latifa received the signal. She was to hold her mouth shut and not a word was to pass her now quivering lips.

All was silent. Latifa noticed Zaida sob. She clearly was the only one in the room who truly cared for Latifa's mother. Latifa's father, on the other hand, took a cigarette out of his Phirran and lit it. Latifa's face turned crimson, her eyebrows shot up and she raged out of the room. She climbed the next set of stairs to the second floor where her room had been.

It was a rather ragged room and the only room that had survived the disastrous floods. Since it was cleaner than the other rooms, it proved to be the most suitable place for her mother to rest, well, till her dea...

While entering the room Latifa stumbled near the door but soon managed to maintain her balance. She noticed her mother awake in her bed. It was the sound of the stumble that had woken her mother up.

'Lati... Latifa *jaan*,' her mother whispered. Her voice was mild and rather timid. It took great effort for her to utter even a single word.

'Amai,' Latifa replied as she lit a candle and sat beside her. Her mother did not say anything for a long time and stared at the ceiling while Latifa only wondered what the next step would be. While her thoughts battled with each other, where one 'right' struck the other 'wrong' down, she completely lost the track of time. She did not want to lie. She could not speak the truth either and after giving it enough thought she decided to stay mum. It was difficult for her to make any decisions. It is in these moments of our lives when lies seem so calming and soothing to ones ears.

Her mother too did not utter a word and it seemed as if, in the silence, both were communicating in their own way. Latifa remembered the time when she had been the one in bed while her mother had very tactfully taken care of everything. Even though Latifa had been diagnosed with a mild fever, her mother had not left her side of the bed and had spent hours caressing Latifa's arm. Everything was coming back to her, all the memories. She held her mother's hand tight in hers and very gently kissed it. Completely lost in her own world, Latifa did not even realize Zaida joining her. Latifa hugged her as well. Zaida had in her hands a bowl filled with hot soup, perhaps one of the last ones that would be cooked in the house.

She held out the spoon, blew it once or twice and tried to serve it to Latifa's mother who was now murmuring some old prayer under her breath. It had been an old habit of hers.

'Baji, I have made this soup for you,' Zaida said politely. As Zaida continued serving Latifa's mother, Latifa's focus shifted to Zaida's hands that had gotten all too bony and raw.

'Latifa *jaan*, go have dinner. Amijan is waiting for you,' Zaida said.

'They've not been giving you any food. Haven't they?' Latifa replied completely ignoring what Zaida had just asked. She continued staring at Zaida's scraped hands.

'Shh!!' cried Zaida, hiding her hands from Latifa.

'Don't ever say that *jaana*,' she peeped towards the door and continued. 'It's all lies. I'm perfectly al...'

'I won't go without you this time,' interrupted Latifa.

'All the worlds will run out of food and I will still be the last person to have some. *Jaana* don't worry about me. Go have your dinner,' Zaida replied instantly.

'But?'

'Shh...' Zaida blinked twice. 'Just go and let me serve this hot soup to your mother. I am perfectly alright,' she lied and simply forged a smile on her face. She had very tidy locks and Latifa always admired her rosy cheeks that were now marked with scratches. Latifa held on to her knees for a little while and without any further utterance left the room.

Downstairs the dinner had already been served on a sheet (*dastar-khwan*) and after a very brusque dinner, in what seemed like the last candlelight they would have in days, Latifa paused and thanked God for the shelter they had, for the food she just ate.

'It doesn't harm to be thankful to God for a change,' she thought to herself as she shot a gaze at her father who was literally hogging over his food. Her grandmother on the other hand kept on serving food in his already full plate. She couldn't stand the sight of either of them and had long foreseen the dark shadows that pondered over their consciousness.

'May God guide them and help them realize their mistake,' Latifa prayed under her breath, dashing out of the room. She was a firm believer of the unseen world and the life beyond what we foolish people call death. Aged only fourteen, she had grabbed onto these 'life-lessons' very well.

When she entered her room, Zaida had finished feeding her mother and was already near the door when Latifa took out some vegetables wrapped in bread out from her pocket. She held it out to Zaida who initially rejected the offer, but just as her hunger paved in, she accepted the bread. Her hands shivered and her cheeks grew evermore red. With a smile on her face, Zaida hugged Latifa who was taken aback by the gesture.

'You would have done the same,' Latifa said, tightening her hug. In the midst of all the melodrama a few noises came from downstairs. Latifa realized it was her grandmother who continuously kept calling out for Zaida, cursing her and humiliating her in the course.

'*Hata Jaanmarga*! Where are you? Come Down!!' cried Latifa's grandmother on top of her voice.

Zaida flustered. All the colour that was left in her soul suddenly left her body. She held her scathed hand out, stroked Latifa's cheek with her finger and paced out of the room.

Latifa's attention now fell on her mother. Her mother's skin was pale and was covered with red spots. Latifa fell to the ground right beside the bed, and cupped her mother's hands within hers.

'Pray. Pray,' she thought to herself, for prayers alone could help her now. Latifa could hear Zaida being slapped, once, then the second time, and then the third. She shut her eyes tight as tears began pouring out of her eyes uncontrollably. Misery had long befallen on her house and was now only completing its job. She began thinking of all the happy moments of her life, a time when all was well and all her miseries had gone out for a holiday, a long holiday indeed. Visions!

Everything went blank... no, she saw something... She now saw herself with her mother who was helping her cross the road... Her father locking her in her room... Uncle Gul with her favourite sweets in his decrepit hands... Her dreams dreaming in the dream... and blank again.

. . . .

CHAPTER 2

Something moved. Latifa woke up and to her surprise realized that she had accidentally fallen asleep.

It was still dark outside. Latifa realized that it was her mother's hand that had moved, that had woken her up. There was a candle lit beside the bed and was the only source of light in the room.

'The Hands Moved!' Latifa exclaimed. She looked at her mother and saw her eyes slightly open.

'Amai?' she uttered as her mouth felt completely dry.

'Are you all right? What is it?' she asked, repeatedly shaking her mothers tender hands.

'I was ju... I was just won-der-ing...' Latifa's mother whispered. Her voice was weak and sounded drab. It was clear that it took great effort for her to get words out of her mouth.

'Amai, what do you mean?' Latifa asked, narrowing her eyes while her mother only stared at the ceiling.

Outside, the winds began to blow shaking the wooden windows with great force. A hen's call could be heard from a distance and the candle, Latifa noticed, was about to burn out.

Her mother tried to lift herself up but all her attempts failed, until Latifa herself assisted her. Her mother's hair was sticking out from all directions and dark circles now resided under her eyes. No matter how tired Latifa's mother looked or how weak she had gotten, her eyes still sparkled the same as ever. Latifa remembered how once her mother had spoken to her about the 'magic' of one's eyes, how one can judge a person by the shine in their eyes. Yes, the shine. In her mother's eyes she could see a better future, a future with no misery and only happiness. Her mother mustered all her strength and tried to speak.

'You've been so strong, *jaana*,' she said, kissing Latifa's hands. Latifa smiled as her eyes watered in pride. Soon, she felt tears running down her raw cheeks, finding their way down her slender neck. Oh yes, those tears that leave their mark on the skin, for they are so strong and so full of emotions.

'N... Now before I depart...' Latifa's mother fumbled.

'Don't say that,' Latifa intruded, hugging her mother tight.

Her mother gently caressed Latifa's hair. She had firm belief in Latifa and she certainly had not loved any soul more that she had loved her.

'Not saying it won't make it any easier *jigar*,' Latifa's mother said.

'I have something very important that I need to give you, but before I do that...' she paused, '...you must listen to me very carefully,' Latifa's mother sounded impatient.

'I have very little time *jaana*,' she whispered. 'There is a box un... under the bed, jus...just take it out.'

Latifa very brusquely began searching for the box and found it stuck under the lopsided bed. It was only after repeated attempts that she was finally able to pull it out. She pulled it out and firmly placed it on her mother's lap.

Latifa's mother held on to the box for a little while. Her eyes twinkled as she saw the wooden handcrafted box again. She continued gawking at it as if time had gone still, as if she had found all the happiness in her life.

'*Jaana*,' she said with evermore hurry.

'Th...This box contains one of the m... most precious gifts I've ever received in my life.' As she opened the box her eyes widened and her face lit with a smile.

The box contained a bright red coloured cloth that had been very carelessly folded. Soon Latifa realized that this cloth wasn't something she had never seen before. She wore it every day. In fact she was wearing one right now. It was a Phirran.

As Latifa felt the cloth with her fingers, she wondered what it was made of, for she had never seen any Phirran made of such silky material. And the colour, oh, how could she miss out on the colour, for it was so vibrant, so full of life. She was so consumed by the beauty of the Phirran that she could barely pay attention to the surroundings. She was brought back to her senses when she heard a loud thud near the footsteps.

Her mother too glanced at the door but no one seemed to be there. Ignoring the sound, she quickly returned to where she had left the conversation. As she continued, she looked straight into Latifa's eyes.

'Now Lis... Listen to me,' she said as her voice drove into to a whisper.

'This Phirran is no normal Phirran. It belonged to a queen, the third queen of Maharaja Hari Singh.'

Latifa gulped in disbelief while her mother only smiled. Latifa's mother had always enjoyed narrating stories and as she was preparing for her departure, she wanted to leave Latifa with her last tale.

'It's true *Jaana*,' she said, nodding. 'But...but she wasn't able to find it.'

Her mother peeped at the door one more time. Latifa could see the sadness in her eyes; she could feel the pain that resided in her mother's heart but she did not quite understand what her mother was trying to say.

'Just I...like me. Only your great grandmother, who had stolen it from the royal household, had been able to unravel the mystery behind this Phirran. Your grandmother failed...' She paused.

'... and I failed too,' she said regretfully.

'Find what *amai*?' Latifa asked as her eyes began to twitch in curiosity.

'Find What?'

'The secret *jaana*. The magic that resides and stays hidden be...behind this Phirran,' she said, clawing the Phirran.

'But you m...must *Jaana*, this Phirran,' she said, holding the Phirran out. 'This Phirran can rob the richest of the rich; can help the poorest of the poor. It can hide anything, be it gold coins or a locket and can store as much as it can in its pockets. The gold threads that have been used to embellish the cloth can provide one with the most exhilarating heat and its hood, oh yes *jaana*, its hood...' she paused as her smile returned.

'It can make one...'

'One what Amai?' Latifa asked impatiently.

'Invisible!'

Latifa gasped. Her eyes widened as wide as they could get. She could not believe it. All this information was heavy to take in and she wanted to quickly store it but her mother did not stop there. She wanted to make the most of the little time she was left with. 'But jigar, be careful for only the true beholder of this Phirran shall know the secret. The greedy shall die and the careless might never get a chance to say goodbye. With every new owner shall come a new secret.'

Latifa tried her level best to absorb everything her mother had just revealed. The candle was about to burn out while the sun was preparing its entrance for a new day.

'I trust you with this small gift *myon jigar.*'

She held Latifa's hand and looked her straight in the eye.

'And I know that you are ready. I love you more than anything in this worl...'

Crash! Latifa shot back to have a better look at the door. It seemed as if the cats had yet again found their way into the house. As she turned back she saw her mother's eyes shut in peace. Slowly, very slowly, the grip with which she had held Latifa's hand loosened. As Latifa's mother sighed her last breath, the calls for the Morning Prayer began outside and continued till the candle actually burned out.

....

CHAPTER 3

All was still. Even the sound of her own heart-beat seemed alien to her and it felt as if all that she had known up till this moment, all the knowledge that she had gained just vanished in thin air. It felt as if she were to start everything afresh. Was it a new beginning or a dead end, she could not say. All that she did know was that the only person who had given her a reason to live had just passed away.

She lay shattered on the bedside and in her hand shone her new gift. Well, she sure had to pay a heavy price for this 'wondrous' Phirran.

What a fine embroidered Phirran it was. Latifa, in her motionless state, stared outside the window. She observed the path of the sunrays but had no desire to stand in it.

There were still so many things left unclear. Was it safe to wear the Phirran without knowing the secret? Would it harm people who touch it? How was she to unravel the mystery? Could she tell anyone else about it? All these questions bombarded her brain and she felt helpless, as the only source of all the answers had now gone for a leave, a long leave indeed.

Latifa rummaged for the prayer mat from a wardrobe and began praying *Fajr*. In the silence Latifa continued praying with all her heart. With knees bent down, hands cupped together and eyes feebly shut in prayer, Latifa concentrated on all that her mother had shared with her. Apart from the new Phirran, one of the dearest gifts that her mother had left behind was this art of praying and Latifa wished to continue it till her last breath. She folded the Phirran carefully inside the wooden box and hid it in its place.

'I will return,' she whispered. Just as she reached the door she turned back. 'Good Bye, Amai. May God guide you for the rest of your journey too,' she prayed as she finally left the room.

It was heart wrecking to break the news to the rest of the residents of the house, for every time she told anyone, her mother's death would seem even more real, realer than she had wanted it to be. She still had not learnt to confront what we call 'the ugly truth'.

The burial took place the very next morning at the nearest **Kabristan.** Not many people attended it, but those who did turn up, Latifa saw through her window, were very kind and sympathetic. All the roads in and out of Srinagar were still blocked and thus it was difficult to spread the word of Latifa's mothers' demise to other relatives. Thus only two people truly mourned, herself and Zaida, while her father and her grandmother kept themselves busy hiding all the gold Latifa's mother had owned.

A few days passed away but not much happened. Every evening Latifa would manage to grab some time and pay a visit to her little secret. She had still not tried the Phirran on as she feared it might explode, or, something unimaginable would happen. Every time she would touch the Phirran she would feel happiness and warmth flow through her veins. Just as she would hear the chirps of the evening birds, she would quickly pack the Phirran up and hide it again.

'It must've been really dear to the queen,' she thought one day as she stroke the golden embroidery. It always felt great to hold the Phirran, for she would feel powerful touching it.

Ever since her encounter with the divine Phirran, Latifa always had the urge to share her secret with someone, with Zaida, at least. She was certain that her mother had firm belief in her, not that her mother had cautioned her not to tell the secret to anyone.

As night approached, clouds began to surround the city and as the last specter of light vanished behind the Himalayas the first raindrops fell. Thunder cracked!

'*Myano Khudayo!* It's back!' Cried Latifa's grandmother while she stared at the ceiling. 'Wasn't it enough the last time?'

It was an old habit of hers, of very conveniently sliding the blame on someone else. This time it was God Himself who had to deal with this mindless beast. It was ironic that she was not the only one blaming God, for the whole town was perplexed. Everyone was peeping out of his or her windows, scared to death at the very sight of the rain. The wound of the recent floods was still fresh in everyone's memories. With every rumble of the lightening someone or the other in the house shuddered.

As Latifa finished her dinner, she hastily pocketed some raw vegetables and bread and made her way to the attic, a tiny room right next to her's. She paused after every step she took and thought twice. She was still doubtful about sharing the secret with Zaida but finally made up her mind to vomit the secret out.

The attic room was somewhat dark and dingy. While water continuously leaked from the ceiling, cobwebs had homed the corners of each wall. As Latifa neared the door she could hear someone sob. Zaida had been crying. Just as Latifa entered the room she noticed Zaida turn the other way as if trying to hide something. Latifa very quietly neared her and hugged her from behind.

'We are in this together,' Latifa said very fluently in Kashmiri, turning Zaida around. She could truly feel Zaida's helplessness.

'**Wadun ma hya**. You make me cry too,' Latifa said, holding out the napkin with some bread and vegetables wrapped in it. Zaida was given food only once a day and that too with minimal portions and it gave enough reasons for Latifa to hoard food for her every night.

'Dont cry, please,' Latifa repeated.

'Oh *Jaana* it was just nothing. Something went into my...'

'You were the one who would tell me to be brave and now look at you,' Latifa wiped Zaida's tears and strengthened her hug. She suddenly remembered the work she had come here for.

'Now listen to me, I need to tell you something,' she said, trying to sit on the naked cold floor. '...but ***Allah-ki-kasam hai*** don't tell anyone.'

In the darkness she could not see Zaida properly but that wasn't even important for the conversation she was to have with her, for her trust rested in Zaida's pure heart, the same heart that had guided Latifa through her ups and downs.

Downstairs, Latifa's grandmother finished hogging her food. She found the perfect time to share something so important that delaying it would only be useless on her part. It was the perfect moment she could find in days. The rain was loud and Latifa, she knew, had gone upstairs to feed Zaida. Tonight as her hawk eyes gave a different sparkle. She smirked and began with an evil glint in her eyes.

'***Hato jigra. Tse ha khyot na kiheen,*** eat *jigar*, I've made this delicacy specially for you,' she said compassionately as she continued serving some more of the mixed vegetables on his plate. Fresh supplies of food and candles had reached them but they were still just as ungrateful.

'There is something I mean to tell you jigra,' she said looking around as if crosschecking for any eavesdroppers. She wanted to be alone with her son for this precious conversation.

The rains now bashed against the windows and its sound made the candles flicker. This was the perfect time, the perfect moment.

'It's about that *jaan-e-marg* wife of yours,' she gulped. 'I've been trying to tell this to you since so long but the time *jaana*, the time, it's never right.'

'But what is it?' Latifa's father asked in anticipation. He grabbed the food in his hand and stuffed it in his mouth. He seemed to take keen interest in the fresh gossip that was to follow.

'That morning *jaana*, that very morning, she...' she began as her words raced their way out of her mouth.

Latifa's father lay still, his eyes wide open and waited for his mother to complete this lifelong tail that seemed to have no end. He only waited.

'What is it?' Zaida asked earnestly.

'Tel...' she swallowed the food and continued. 'Tell me, **Khuda-pak ki kasam,** I won't let it slip to another soul.'

'Shh, you are too loud!' she cautioned Zaida even though the rains were literally bashing against the roof overhead.

'Well then tell me,' said Zaida, completely ignoring Latifa's pleas.

Latifa let out a heavy sigh. Now was the time, she thought to herself. Her heart pounded hard against her chest. She shushed all the thoughts that were bothering her at the moment, pressed her hand against her chest and blurted out.

'No one knows about this. No one...'

'What?' Zaida interrupted.

'On the...' Latifa hesitated. 'On the morning of Amma's...' she paused, pressing her eyes and continued. 'De... Death,' she finally managed. 'She gave me a present.'

Zaida's eyes widened. 'What kind of present?' she asked.

'She gave me a Phirran but it is no normal Phirran...' She gulped. 'It has been embroidered with threads made of real gold.'

'Wow!' exclaimed Zaida. Like any other Kashmiri girl she too had once dreamt of a Phirran, not the normal one but the one that the prince's gifted their wives. Before Zaida could roll deeper into her fantasy world, Latifa barged in.

'But there is more to it,' Latifa whispered. Her heart battered from within and she couldn't keep pace with her breathing. Now was that impeccable juncture that would finally set her free of her self-doubt; she would now know if all of this was a dream or not, if she had been fooled by her own mother or not.

'I had always known it *jaana*. That **Shikas** wife of yours was hiding something and she made sure to keep it a secret.'

Latifa's father frowned.

'That morning *jigar*,' she said impatiently. 'Right before the stroke of her death, your wife gave your daughter something. She told Latifa something for real *jaana*, I heard it on my own.'

She shushed Latifa's father before he could even open his mouth to speak, and continued. Outside, the rains lightened a bit but the robust winds blew with the same strength.

'Aaa... before you say anything *jigar*, hear me out. From behind the curtains, I saw that old sheep give Latifa a box, a wooden box!' she exclaimed.

'But Ama...'

'Patience, *jaana*, be patient. I have searched the box a million times but nothing; there is nothing in it. Perhaps Latifa *jaan* is hiding something from us.' With these words she finally felt empty. She had held this conversation for so long that now that she had finally been able to blurt it out, she felt free.

'Amai said that there is some kind of magic, some supernatural power that resides in the Phirran,' Latifa said rather innocently.

'She said that I, the only rightful owner can unlock it's secret.'

'What? Are you alright Jaana?' Zaida asked, sounding concerned.

'And... and she said that the secret changes with every beholder.'

'Latifa...'

'and...'

'Latifa, your mother believed in you and just because she used the word magic does not really mean that it carries magic. Your mother was a brave woman and I'm sure that she had meant something else. For her everything was magic, everything was a gift from God. She believed in her dreams and with that in herself. Latifa *jaan*, just as beauty lies in the eyes of the beholder, magic lies in the blood of only those who believe in it.'

'But... but she said it very clearly. I have seen the gold glow with my own eyes. It's real!' she cried.

'She told me very clearly,' Latifa whispered as Zaida comforted her. Silence.

His eyes turned red, he banged his fist on the plate spilling the food on the carpet.

'*Jaana*, do you remember how we would wonder how that hag's family was somewhat well off? This is it! Our answers lie in that box and even though we can't see it, she sure can.' Latifa's grandmother smirked.

Her father's eyes were close to popping out. Had his own daughter betrayed him too? Wrinkles crossed his forehead. He smashed the glass of water against the wall while Latifa's grandmother jumped to her feet in shock. Outrage followed.

'LATIFAAAAA!!!' he shouted.

. . . .

CHAPTER 4

As Latifa heard her father shout, a chill ran down her spine. What could it have been, Latifa thought, that had made her father shout so loud? What indeed?

It seemed as if everything around her stopped. Everything. Only the sound of the raindrops resonated in her ears and slowly the sound grew louder. She remembered the last time her father had shouted so loud. That day Latifa had gone out to her friend's home and had forgotten to cover her head with a scarf. In outrage her father had locked her in her room for two days straight.

She stared into the darkness as if the time had gone still. Some sort of music started playing in her ears but she didn't shut her ears. This ancient lullaby seemed comforting to her ears and she did not want it to stop.

'Won't you go?!!!' Zaida shook Latifa back and forth bringing her back to the unembellished reality. Latifa blinked twice.

She shot up and galloped her way down the stairs, praying under her breath. Zaida too followed Latifa, giving her company.

Her father was staring out the window. Outside, the rains had reduced to mild drizzles and the clouds began giving way to the moonlight. The **dastar-khwan** was still laid out right in the middle of the room and her grandmother was collecting the spilled food, pretending as if she had nothing to do with what would follow next.

Latifa waited near the door. She tightened her scarf, her sign of nervousness, and waited for a response.

'What is in the box?' her father asked abruptly, still staring out the window. He folded his hands but did not look at her. Scared, Latifa did not know how to react to the question. Her heartbeat escalated and her breathing sped up. She simply went blank.

'Wh... What box Abbu?' she hesitantly asked. Her father looked her in the eyes then turned to his mother and began laughing hysterically.

'She doesn't know where the box is,' he said, laughing harder. Latifa noticed a glass in his hand and before she could even see what it was filled with her father smashed it onto the floor. The glass shattered into pieces and piled with the debris of the glass he had shattered earlier.

'You don't know anything about the box huh?' he shouted as he got up. Veins popped on his forehead and his neck. Every step he took closer to Latifa made her more nervous. Her feet trembled and her mouth went dry. Behind her, Zaida surreptitiously held Latifa's hand.

Latifa glanced at her grandmother and knew exactly what had happened. In the deepest of her thoughts she could picture the morning of her mother's demise, she could picture her grandmother eavesdropping on them from behind the curtains. She remembered the awful feeling she felt of someone staring at her from behind. It wasn't the cats after all.

'Latifa Jaan,' her father began and she instantly looked at him. He was only feet away from her. For the first time in her life she felt insecure. Any moment now and she would be slapped right across her face.

'Tell me about the box. What is in it?'

'Nothing Abbai it's just...' Latifa began crying.

'Don't lie!' her father shouted.

'Abbai, It was only a present from Amai. It contains a Phirran, nothing else,' Latifa sobbed.

'Just an embroid... AAAh!!!' Out of nowhere a beastly hand pushed her. Latifa stumbled and hit her head against the wall. Her father, her own *abba* had attacked her. Where had all the love gone? Was she no more her daughter?

'Urg!' her father shouted in frustration.

'Zaida!' he called out. 'Go get the box.'

Zaida entered the room and fixed her eyes at the ground. She herself had just received information about the existence of such a box. Now, how on earth was she to know where Latifa had hid it? She had no choice. While she continued staring at a hole in the carpet, Latifa's father grew impatient.

'What happened?' he shouted.

'But Bhaijan,' she began. 'I am just as unaware of the box as you are. I am clueless as to where the box has been kept or what it contains. May Allah bless you with a long life, but please be kind to Latifa. She has already gone through a lot. Please Bhaij...' she paused. Latifa's father took a step closer to her. He slid his belt out and began hitting Zaida with it.

'But... but *bhaijan*, I don't know anythi...' Zaida shouted in despair. Latifa almost leapt at her father getting into his way.

'Stop Abbai!' she shouted spreading her arms like an eagle. 'She has nothing to do with it.'

Latifa helped Zaida up, who seemed utterly perplexed, and made up her mind.

'I will get the box,' she said respectfully. 'But please leave Zaida alone,' she wrapped her right arm around Zaida's shoulder, walked her out of the room and made her sit on the staircase. Just as she made her way up to her room, Zaida held her hand.

'You don't have to do this *Jaana*. It's yours!' Zaida whispered, sounding desperate. Latifa knew she did not really have a choice. She looked straight at Zaida, gave a genuine smile and made her way to the room.

Everything was swirling in Latifa's head and it gave her a headache. The changes that the past hour had brought in her life were highly unanticipated. She hastily got the handcrafted wooden box out from under the bed and carefully made her way down the steps.

'He would not be able to do anything to it,' she reassured herself. She looked up, prayed the last time and made her way back into the room. She dropped the box in front of her father and from the corner of the room her grandmother joined them too.

'Huh!' her father smirked, 'now you will remember everything,' he said, cracking his knuckles. The sound of her father cracking his knuckles had always made Latifa uncomfortable and she would end up shutting her eyes in disgust.

'Open it up,' her grandmother said. The sparkle in her eyes had returned and she kept her toad-like head held high as if she was the queen herself. Latifa got down to her knees and just as she opened the box, Latifa's grandmother gasped. Whenever her grandmother had checked the box it had been empty but today she could see the magnificent Phirran through her own eyes.

'But it wasn't... how did...?' she stuttered.

'Show it to me!' she held out her aged hands, snatched the Phirran and rubbed it against her cheeks.

'Ah, it is so soft!' she whispered, gently running her fingers across the embroidery that covered the top portion of the cloth and very delicately rolled down to the sides of the sleeves. There really was something magical about the Phirran and it made everyone feel pleasant and happy. It was very unusually attractive.

Her father grabbed it out of her Grandmother's hands, who herself was rather shocked by the gesture, and began searching its pockets. He checked the Phirran from top to bottom but couldn't find anything.

'Where is it?' he asked, raising his voice.

'What Abbai?' she asked earnestly. How much had her grandmother exaggerated?

'Don't act so innocent!' her grandmother snapped. 'I heard everything that morning, the morning your mother died,' she smirked. Latifa could not control it anymore. Pain struck her right in the heart this time and she was deeply hurt. She looked at her father for mercy but he only looked away.

'Latifa! Tell us what this Phirran contains,' he asked, lowering his voice.

'Abbai, I don't know,' she whimpered. 'All that Mother told me was that it belonged to the Maharaja's queen and that it had a secret that even she could not find...'

'Lies!!' her grandmother shouted.

'I am not lying,' Latifa's cheeks turned red and her eyes shot open in rage. She completely lost her temper.

'And even if I knew,' she continued, 'I would rather die than tell you about it.'

'How dare you!' her father screamed, raising his hand in an attempt to slap her. Latifa's grandmother pulled him back.

Latifa had lost the power to feel hurt or in this case even get hurt. The fantasy world she had been living in for years had transformed into a living hell. She knew she was on her own now. Her blood began to boil and she lost all control over her mouth.

'I don't know. I don't know!' She cried. Now, there were only two things that mattered to her, Zaida and the Phirran. The Phirran belonged to her and no one had the right to snatch it away from her or even set eyes on it.

'It's mine!' she shouted, running towards the Phirran. Her father stopped her and pushed her aside.

'Please Abbai, don't take it away from me, that is the only thing left of her's.'

'If you truly want this, you are going to have to tell us the little secret. Latifa jaan, do understand it is for your own safety. What if it harms you or kills you,' he lowered his voice in an attempt to sound concerned, but Latifa very well knew his intentions.

'But *jaan*,' he continued. 'I give you one day to think. Do reveal the secrets of your precious gift as I truly don't want this treasury of your's go waste. My eyes are too weak to see it in a condition like this. Do tell me *jaan* or I shall burn it and set it free.'

. . . .

CHAPTER 5

'Or I shall burn it and set it free.'

Her father's words pricked her heart. Just like a broken tape recorder, his voice continued echoing in her ears. Locked up in her room, the night passed rather quickly, and she still had not been able to come up with anything. For a change, the morning was somewhat bright and pleasant. Outside, Latifa noticed, new puddles had taken form on the roads.

Her heart felt heavy. Staring at the streets from her window, Latifa could not figure out how she would convince her father later in the evening. One second she would think of running away but she would realize the implications her actions would have on Zaida, and she certainly could not leave without her Phirran. Time literally ran a marathon till the Sun finally set. Anything could happen now. She took out the praying mat that had been folded into a cheroot, laid it out on the floor, and started praying. With her eyes shut, Latifa asked for strength, she asked for relief and she wished for peace.

The last hour too passed instantaneously. In moments of crisis, time is never a friend and no one shall ever be able to befriend it.

She went near the door and was surprised to see it unlocked. As she made her way down the stairs she finally made up her mind as to what she would do now. Truth. She would speak the truth. She did not care even if her own life was at stake but speaking the truth was the best step she could think of. After all, Latifa really did have a very strong and an enduring character.

The last rays of sunlight vanished beyond the mountains and darkness blanketed the city. For some reason Latifa had always found comfort in the dark.

As she entered the room, both her father and grandmother looked at her.

The only source of light in the room was a candle that had been kept near the stove and right beside it lay her precious Phirran, blazing in the silence. Like always, Latifa's father was staring out the window and her grandmother, like a puppet, rattled here and there. Latifa's eyes searched for Zaida but to her surprise she was not present in the room.

'Yes *Jaana*,' her grandmother said, rubbing her hands together.

'Tell us and no one shall harm you anymore. Tell us, for this Phirran could be dangerous for you,' she sounded restless. Greed had conquered her brain and had enslaved her senses.

Latifa's mouth dried, not because she was scared but because she had not had water in a long time. She was no more scared of the future.

'Amijan. I don't know,' she said looking her in the eyes. She did not move, did not utter another word and stood still waiting for a response.

'I have never used the Phirran and perhaps never will, but I would want my Phirran back,' she said bluntly. She could see her father's face turn red.

'Shut up!' he shouted. He grabbed the Phirran in his hand, lit the stove and held the Phirran above the fire.

'Latifa you have one last chance. Tell ME!!!'

The Phirran was only inches away from the fire and its little threads had already begun catching fire. Latifa shifted. She felt her heart skip a beat. Over time the bond she had created with the Phirran had been so strong that she could feel the scorching heat of the fire, even though she stood feet away.

'N... No. Abbai. Please,' she pleaded desperately. The Phirran meant the world to her.

'Please Abbai,' she reiterated and before she could even reach out…Puff!

The enchanted Phirran had been set on fire. Latifa screamed, for her own insides burned too. She held her hands over her head and bent to her knees screaming. She could not bear the agonizing pain. As the burning sensation reached her chest, she felt she would explode any second now.

The pain grew from her chest to her legs till she could bear no more. She wanted to open her eyes but couldn't. She gathered the little strength she had and tried opening her eyes. Her Phirran sure had caught fire but the flame was not of the usual colour. Purple mixed with a tinge of green, the flame grew like a ferocious eagle leaping over its pray. Latifa could not manage a sound but her insides sure were frightened to the skin. The sound of the fire roared in her ears as if she too had caught fire.

Someone whispered in her ears. Someone's soothing voice was trying to communicate with Latifa and it took long enough till Latifa could make out what it was trying to say.

'Do the right thing,' the voice whispered. In the very same instant the excruciating roar in her ears returned. She held both her hands on the floor and tried to lift herself up, but she simply couldn't. It was only in the third or the fourth attempt that Latifa managed to get back on her feet, her newly independent feet.

Fearless, she ran towards the Phirran grabbing it tight and began running towards the door. Midway she realized something absurd. The hotter she had expected the fire to be, the cooler it felt. It seemed as if she had run her hands through ice-cold water. As she made her way through the corridor, down the stairs, she accidentally set fire to the old carpet that covered the floor.

As she reached outdoors she threw the Phirran on the ground. Her heart had never pounded so fast ever before.

'Ahhhhhhh!!!!' someone shrieked from within the house and as she looked back she saw fire raging out of the windows. How was she to save Abba and Amijan, but most importantly, how was she to save Zaida? She knew Zaida must have been locked in the room on the ground floor? Her eyes suddenly fell on the Phirran.

'This could be my only chance,' she thought to herself.

Black smoke was oozing out of the Phirran; however, its colour was still the same. Her eyes drew to the golden embroidery. The golden embroidery? Yes!! It was glowing!!!

'Maybe it's a call to use it,' Latifa thought as she wore the Phirran for the very first time.

The Phirran felt lighter than she had anticipated and at the same time it energized her. The embroidery now grew brighter than ever. She shut her eyes in peace, wore the hood to prevent her hair from burning, and went inside the burning house.

'Abbai? Zaida? Amijan?' she shouted on top of her voice but no response followed. The ceiling above was burning and the huge pillar supporting it was about to break way any moment now.

'Abbai!?' she shouted again.

'Ammijan?!!'

She went near a locked door and banged it hard. She kicked the door and it burst open in the very first go. The smoke completely blocked her sight and was now choking her.

'Zai... Zaida?' Latifa choked. It was getting difficult for her to breathe. She was about to leave the room when in the distance she saw something move.

'Amij... Zaida!!!'

Zaida had collapsed on the floor and was unconscious. Latifa tried to reach Zaida when suddenly a huge wooden log fell, separating Latifa from her. The whole house was about to collapse. She jumped over the sizzling log and held on to Zaida. There was no way out and Latifa did not have any strength left to carry Zaida. Was it the end, the end to her story? Was this the end of her journey with the Phirran?

She kept Zaida's head on her lap and covered it with the Phirran. Half of Zaida's neck was burnt not to miss her hair that had reduced to mere patches covering her head. In her hands, Latifa noticed, lay a piece of paper with burnt corners. She held it in her hands and saw something written in Urdu.

'My Phirran and this piece of paper shall not burn tonight,' she whispered as she shoved the paper in her pocket.

She was not scared, nor was she sad. Throughout the course of her life, she thought, she had learnt so much. All the small things that had once bothered her seemed to fade away from her memory. If she were to die tonight, she was glad that she would die alongside someone she utterly loved. Zaida was her source of joy, her source of hope. Zaida.

A very weird smoky feeling ran across Latifa's body. She felt like being squeezed into nothingness, as if her body was being contracted into a minuscule speck of dust. As the feeling faded away she opened her eyes and was shocked to see herself and Zaida outside the house. Zaida was still in her lap just as she had been.

'Transportation!' she exclaimed under her breath.

'The Phirran can transport!' she smiled, trying to get up. She could save the others. She dragged Zaida to the other side of the road and readied herself to rescue the others. Just as she approached the main gate, Latifa saw the whole house shudder. She stopped. Within moments the whole house collapsed in front of her eyes.

'No!' she yelped, hiding her eyes from the fire. Her father, her grandmother, her house…all was gone.

She looked back at Zaida and realized that she too had not shown any movement in a very long time.

'No, No, No, No, No,' she began running towards her. 'No, No!' she cried harder.

'Zaida?' she shook her body and tried to wake her but Zaida did not show any movement.

In less than a minute she had lost everyone she had loved.

'Zaida,' she cried, burying her face in Zaida's arms. She felt the arm move. She looked at Zaida and saw her cough. Latifa released a deep contended sigh.

'This was G…' Zaida choked. 'This was God's will,' she finally uttered while Latifa listened to her intently. A smile ran across Latifa's face and she kissed Zaida on the cheek. In the distance Latifa could hear men shout.

'No one will believe us, Zaida. They will kill us. We must run and hide somewhere or, or they will take away the Phirran!' she said in haste.

'Don't worry *Jaana*. Everything will be all right…' she paused, 'as long as we have the Phirran,' she said with a smile on her face and Latifa smiled too.

'***Naar! Naar***! Fire!' the voices of the men grew louder. The houses nearby had caught fire too, but fortunately the families that had lived there had left the premises right after the floods.

Latifa could hear the footsteps of the men approach them. She covered Zaida under her Phirran, closed her eyes and swoosh! Both Latifa and Zaida vanished in what we call 'thin air'.

The morning breeze shook the Chinar trees and made the autumn leaves fall loose to the ground. From far away it seemed as if the trees had been set on fire, well, that was the beauty of the Chinar trees.

Under a shed that was supposed to be a bus stand, stood a young girl who wore the most beautiful Phirran anyone had ever seen or even worn. She wasn't alone. A woman with a slightly burnt ear stood next to her with her arms around the young girl. Both had their eyes stuck to one side of the road.

'Are you sure this is the place?' Latifa asked with utmost curiosity as her red scarf waved with the passing wind.

A strange noise suddenly filled the air. Instead of being scared, both of them were relieved.

'It's here,' Zaida said in a rather jolly tone. The noise of the engine grew louder till finally a small red rusty bus approached the stand.

Latifa smiled and got closer to Zaida. The weight of the Phirran was not all that she carried with her. Her heart still mourned the loss of her father.

As the bus neared them, Latifa picked up a bag from the ground and looked at Zaida.

'Where does it go?' Latifa asked.

'Somewhere far away. You will like it,' Zaida replied.

As both of them followed their way through the aisle of seats, all the people kept gawking at the beautiful Phirran. Ignoring them, Latifa and Zaida sat at the very back of the bus.

Zaida too could not keep her eyes off the Phirran. The embroidery reflected the sun's rays all around and at the same time it spread its warmth.

What was the secret to its beauty? Was it the golden embroidery that had been stitched using real gold or was it simply because of the 'true beholder', no one could say.

'It can rob the richest of the rich. Can help the poorest of the poor.'

These words echoed in Latifa's ears and her confusion grew.

'Why did it work?' she asked Zaida.

Confused, Zaida tried to make sense of the words but failed.

'Why did the Phirran work on the night of the fire?' Latifa said hastily as she tied her scarf. Zaida now understood and her frown faded away.

'Ah, *Jaana*, the little I could understand is that…' she coughed and continued, '*Jaana*, the Phirran is the most faithful object I have ever seen in my life. Your mother had known the secret very well but had failed to apply it. The very second she handed the Phirran to you, the Phirran sensed that it had been passed on and changed the key to it.'

Latifa listened to her intently.

'Latifa there is something else in this Phirran. Along with its secret it changes its use too. Your great grandmother used it to hoard the gold from the queen's treasury, however, *Jaana* it has one element that does not change at all and shall never change.'

'What is it?' Latifa asked impatiently.

'It works only when the beholder is in dire need for something. It will succumb to your needs only when you dearly need to use it.'

Latifa finally understood. 'And that is why…'

'…it had worked that fateful night,' Zaida completed.

Latifa wanted to forget the past. She wanted to forget all that had happened and desired to start a new beginning. She intended to forget all her memories of this place, but even if she succeeded, would she be able to erase it from her dreams too? She pondered over the thought for a while then simply gazed out of the window.

She recalled what her mothers riddle had said.

It will help the poorest of the poor and will destroy the greedy from within and from without. This was the magic; this was the universal secret of the Phirran that Latifa had to learn the hard away. And how to use it? Well, that is totally up to you!!!

The End

<u>SO, WHY LIVING?</u>

Have you ever thought of that prickly confusion?
Where your might and sight may fade away.
Is it true that only summers and winters can
Put you through a night-less dream?

My smile widened as I saw yours,
When will I get to see it again?
That tear that falls all so softly,
Pouring down, lifting up, totally free.

For Gods shall never prick the balloon,
They have intentions of bursting it altogether.
For peace shall not find its place here,
And will soar into the blissful skies forever.

So should I dream the dream,
This world is forging on me?
Can I not just sit back and smile,
And explore the world that lies within me?

It pinches, the truth, right into your heart,
The very thought of colorless butterflies.
Or for that matter, an imageless reflection,
Staring at you, gawking at you, unknowingly.

Have not the skies forbidden red?
Have not the suns bequeathed their pride?
Isn't love just a trumpet feeling,
With millions of musical notes, all united?

These musicians fear making mistakes,
For these mistakes are sinful and cannot be forgotten.
These musicians fear being laughed upon,
For their voices mean a lot to them.

Is there any rope stronger than this feeling?
I shall use it to hang what should be squealing,
Choking on, for life or for death,
Till it is set free left breathing.

So, why living?

There has to be a purpose,
This hearty sensation,
Something binds us to this world.
Search for that light, search for the life and remain unbeaten.

So where is it, that holy secret?

A Vacant Death

CHAPTER 1

It was about time. Everything was going just as planned. Far away from her, near the ajar gate, he was playing. His hands swaying in all directions, his legs jumbling at every other step of his, after all, he was only a small child of two or three.

She stared at him from behind the meshed door, watching every step of his. The way he giggled and flashed his smile all around, the way he held himself to maintain his balance on his infant feet.

How vacant could one's death be? There are times when death welcomes those who did never deserve it. They are plunged into the deep well that has no opening or end, into a humungous area between space and time.

She held her breath tight. No sign of fear, no sign of breathlessness, just a calm figure staring at its prey. She had never thought that all of this would be so easy. Just pull a string and there it goes, the drape to one's life, shut forever.

She now had visions, not of worldly creatures but of creatures that never did exist. Somewhere deep inside, her conscience did prick her and for an instant she did sense that what she was doing was wrong but everything slowly faded away as if her vision was being blurred from reality by the ghostly creatures themselves. Is she possessed? Suddenly the thought of her **brother** struck her mind and her visions finally took over her conscience. She was now, as they say, possessed but not by ghosts or by souls but simply by herself. For her, reality was not real anymore and the thought of love was not lovely anymore. Her brother, who now did not exist anymore, stood there staring at her. Oh dear Godly Bassoon, what is happening?

She could not take any of this madness anymore. She shook her head twice and tried to focus on the child who, well, wasn't rightfully hers and certainly would not be after what she was about to do. Very slowly, she opened the door to make up enough space and rolled a bright yellow ball across, in the direction of the boy who was playing near the small rusted gate. The ball rolled across the pathway, missing the boy just as intended, and went out through the gap between the ground and the open gate.

The child's attention diverted to the ball and for a second he stood still. You fool, don't follow the ball! The little boy did exactly as he had been taught. He pushed the ajar gate further and tried to make his way out, chasing after his beloved ball.

'Jajajaja....' he enunciated as he went after the ball. This was all the young soul was capable of saying but the question still remained, would his very first words, or syllables rather, be his last?

At the very back, the woman smiled. Her work for now was done, not complete yet, just done. It would take quite a while to complete her job but her smile conveyed her triumph over her success.

Suddenly the tyres of a car could be heard, screeching against the rough road and a little shake of the ground suggested that there was an accident. Her eyes shrank and her smile widened. The spring air suddenly did not seem as beautiful as it had before, for nature here had taken a sharp turn.

Sitting in his study, with a pen perched in his hand, Dr. Zarg suddenly gazed outside the window, which lay next to his study table. Something flashed outside the window, as if a mix of colours dangling in the free space.

A premonition? Or was it simply his vision that played games?

On his right lay piles of pediatric books he referred to every now and then and in front of him, stacked very neatly, were prescriptions that still needed to be signed. He clearly could not afford to waste any time on leisurely activities, such as thinking, and thus resumed his work. No matter how hard he tried, the much vibrant flash of colours or whatever that it was still occupied most of his brain.

Outside, Dr. Zarg noticed the last streaks of sunlight fade away faster than ever before. Nevertheless, there still was time till proper sundown, whereby he would take a break, join his family for dinner and finally retire to bed.

Having had a long busy week, Dr. Zarg had forgotten the sense of being free. At the moment life, for him, seemed as if a gigantic box only filled with deathly prescriptions that would soon eat him up.

His hands ached and his finger's felt stiff. As he approached the last set of prescriptions his mood lightened a bit. His experienced grey beard had stiffened and the light wrinkles around the ends of his almond eyes were prominent like never before. At such points in time his protruding nose usually gave an itch, which he would utterly distaste. The pile had almost ended when suddenly the sound of someone approaching his study tore the silence apart.

It seemed as if the person climbing the stairs was in some hurry. In a house of four, which included Dr. Zarg's son and a daughter, Dr. Zarg had got accustomed to these loud noises.

The sound grew louder till the door of his study was barged open. In came Surbhi, his wife, as if in a rush. Her slender cheek had grown pale and streaks of sweat were rolling down her forehead. Her heartbeat had a very unsteady rhythm and her chest moved uncontrollably. Something certainly had gone wrong which had made her rush up to his study, a place she hardly ever lay a step in, in such a hurry. For a split second, out of nowhere, Dr. Zarg could feel the flash of light floating in the air but he shook the very thought of it and concentrated on what seemed more important.

Surbhi did not say anything for a long while. Her hazel eyes sparkled a sense of trouble and her face expression gave out most of what she wanted to convey, just that she could not gather the right words to express herself. She gathered her breath and finally managed. 'It's little Ahmed,' she panted as her shock driven tone resonated within the thin walls of the study.

'You must go! It is the Naqash family,' she paused, gulped her fears and continued, 'they need you.' At this point she shut her eyes. Even though Dr. Zarg heard her clearly he still sensed ambiguity in what she wanted to convey. For one thing, the Naqash family had been somewhat close to Dr. Zarg and it was not their seeking help that astounded Dr. Zarg but the mention of little Ahmed, Naqash's son, which made him uncomfortable.

'But what happened?' Dr. Zarg finally uttered. 'What about little Ahmed?'

His wife looked him straight into his eyes as if trying to convey a complex code.

'An accident!' she whispered and a tear rolled out from her fear-stricken eyes, delicately rounding her cheek, down her neck.

Terror ran through Dr. Zarg's spine. He remembered it was only last week that he had seen his children playing with the three year old chap. Shabnam, Dr. Zarg's daughter, had been playing with the spring dandelions and his son, Habib had been running with little Ahmed, chasing after the butterflies. It all seemed so vivid, as if a movie was being projected behind his screens. He could picture the whole seen all over again with the sunlight beaming through the tall Chinar trees and the sweet smell of the flowers rejuvenating his inner self. It all seemed so real but suddenly his imagination took a steep dip as if plunging into a deep pool of nothingness and everything turned dark. Instantaneously he imagined his children being robbed off their smiles and now darkness invaded the scene. In the corner he could now see little Ahmed tied with sticks, crying his throat out and…

'*Jaana* go or else…' Surbhi paused, incapable of completing the sentence. Dr. Zarg jerked his head and shut his eyes in attempt to concentrate on what his wife was trying to say. 'Or else it will be too late.' Surbhi managed, sobbing.

With another jerk in his head, Dr. Zarg made sure he was back in the present. For a moment he felt lost in the gap between reality and fiction but slowly everything started making sense. He himself realized the delicacy of every other second that ticked. He heaved himself from his chair, pushed the pile of books to one corner and began stuffing his usual 'doctor appliances' in his strap bag. His doctor kit included a professional stethoscope, some paramedics, and pairs of scissors, some bandages and a few straps of cotton.

Outside, the wind ruffled and the spring air bequeathed its special charm all around. Dr. Zarg hastily crossed his wife and descended down the narrow staircase. As he flipped open the door, from nowhere, the thought of that ominous flash yet again struck his consciousness and he, like a spectator, commended its beauty.

He rushed through the first street, tightened the grip of his strap bag and followed through the path till he reached the very end. The traffic in the roads was remotely less. Ignoring the street dogs that were playing in one corner, he took a sharp right and continued pacing the road till finally he stopped near a small rusted iron gate. Beyond this very gate a life was at stake.

The gate was rather old and its colour had faded away. It had the typical touch of beautification that all the gates around had, yet there was something that set it apart from the others. Dr. Zarg could already feel the air around him get heavy. Even though the day was about to come to an end, orange streaks of sunlight still danced around in the marvelous sky.

He pushed his strap bag to one side, an involuntary behavior he had adapted over time and began looking for a switch or a bell he could ring. Seeing none, he proceeded to turn the knob of the gate but the knob just did not seem to budge from its place. It was only after due efforts when finally the knob gave in and the gate crept open.

As he entered, everything around him seemed different. The structure of the house was somewhat different and the garden that was on his right definitely seemed bigger and better maintained than his own. Very elegantly he made his way through the pavement trying to ignore the incredible beauty of the magnificent garden, however, as he reached midway he caught a glimpse of someone seated near the extravagantly beautified rose beds. From the house came desperate calls of someone instructing something but Dr. Zarg could not comprehend anything. No matter how loud it was inside the house, no sound really seemed to bother the figure perched near the flowerbeds. In the growing darkness, Dr. Zarg could not figure out who it was until finally he noticed a scarf swaying around the figure's neck and it hit him, 'Yasmeen!'.

Still confused, Dr. Zarg did not disturb her. She must have her own reasons of being outside than with her son upstairs, he thought. As he quickly crossed the pavement he only wondered how one could perfect to stay so motionless. Not giving her much thought, he rang the doorbell hurriedly. Seeing no response, Dr. Zarg began to bang the meshed door until finally the latch of the door clicked and the door opened.

An old woman, Dr. Zarg guessed was Yasmeen's mother-in-law, stood near the door. Dressed in what seemed to be a traditional nightgown, she motioned Dr. Zarg in.

'Oh Doctor, do get in.' Her voice carried a distinct charm and every word of hers felt heavy.

'How is your grandson?' Dr. Zarg asked with utmost concern. With the many emergencies he had already been successful with, this one seemed somewhat different.

The old lady crossed him and went past through a doorway to the other room. Her nightgown seemed too long for her or maybe she was a little too short.

'He has been laid down to rest upstairs, Doctor,' she said, nearing the staircase. 'The other doctor is already trying his level best, but doctor,' she turned and paused for a while. Her brown eyes had an enigmatic obscurity within them and her face revealed everything, both her misery and her helplessness.

'That doctor is no good. My Ahmed is just not okay,' she continued as a tear trickled down. 'Please save my little *jaan*.' she said, her voices as desperate as ever. She held her hand out and motioned Dr. Zarg to follow the stairs. 'They are in the room to the right,' she signaled.

Dr. Zarg ascended the stairs till he reached the dark wooden door. As he opened it all the chaotic voices rushed in his ears.

The room, as he had expected, was filled with a few relatives and a doctor who stood near a haphazard bed in the corner. Little Ahmed had been laid down to rest on the bed. His body had severe cuts and his legs seemed swollen. Most of his head was covered with a white Band-Aid and his face, with blood. The very first sight of Little Ahmed's body ran a shiver down Dr. Zarg's guts and his eyes gave a sudden twitch.

In the room the only person Dr. Zarg could recognize was Jahangir, the father of little Ahmed. He was a sturdy middle-aged man whom Dr. Zarg considered his 'close friend'. His dark locks hid most of his forehead and dangled down till his eyes. A dark black beard played across his face and was rather well maintained. However, it was clear that today he himself was in much of a shock. Dr. Zarg hastily shook Jahangir's hand and very professionally announced, 'I would request everyone to move out immediately. The lesser the people we have in this room the better,' and within seconds the extra lot filed out, each hugging Jahangir as they left the room.

'No time to lose,' Dr. Zarg whispered to himself. His experienced hands got sweaty and at constant intervals, shivered too. He quickly placed his bag on the carpeted floor and rummaged his stethoscope out.

Dr. Zarg got down to his knees and began examining the body for a pulse, but there was none. In the silence that was now piercing his ears, all he wished for was a tiny sound that would set him free and allow him to heave a sigh of relief. Soon he realized that in this world of ours wishes and all the litter share the same fate. He tried repositioning the tail of the stethoscope in search of the tiniest heartbeat, but there simply was no response. In his mind he prayed and prayed, he prayed for that beat that would finally certify that the soul had not left it's premises. As time passed by, while the world continued to run the way it was, no beat followed. He tried the C.P.R but still there was no sign.

'What all have you already tried?' he asked the other doctor who seemed clueless as to how he should respond. He simply stared at the floor like a school kid when asked a tricky question.

'We fixed his marks first,' he suddenly replied 'and also cleaned his woun...'

'That is correct!' Dr. Zarg snapped. 'But first you check for breathing or pulse, as it is the basic component to ones life! You first check that the body gets the right amount of Oxygen!'

He tried his stethoscope again and again but still no beat occurred, no wind blew out in the open sky and no soul did return. He closed his eyes and soon he himself went blank. A faint mix of light flashed and soared across the majestic darkness beneath his eyelids. He slowly lifted his head, staring at the roof and whispered, 'there it goes.'

Behind him he could picture Jahangir's face, a face struck with utter sadness, the face of a lonely father craving for his only son's return. It was in these moments of life that Dr. Zarg hated his job, not because of the criticism of the people but because of the failure one faces throughout the career. For a second he felt responsible for little Ahmed's demise. 'Perhaps I could have saved him,' he thought to himself.

Very silently, Dr. Zarg took out a sketchbook and a pencil from his leather bag and began sketching the body. For a detailed study, sketching always worked well for him. His skill to sketch, as people always told him, was a gift from above. Every stroke of his hand on the paper was so accurate and so perfect that at times taking a picture would seem useless. His sketches would display everything, every single detail that at times even the normal eye could not see.

Dr. Zarg stood up and as he did his knee joints stiffened. He turned around only to find Jahangir awestruck and crying in the corner. Outside, the winds cried too and the moonlight revealed parts of the garden.

'Jahangir?' Dr. Zarg said, getting closer. 'Your son has found his place in heaven. Don't worry for him,' he paused for a moment waiting for a response. 'Carry on with your life and do know that no matter what, I will always be there for you,' he finally concluded.

He helped Jahangir get up and guided him downstairs, his arms very compassionately hung around Jahangir's shoulder and it seemed as if two long lost friends were taking a stroll. Jahangir staggered in the beginning and at times would just stop, staring at the floor, but after much effort they finally reached downstairs. Everyone had already been assembled in the living room, holding on to their breaths in anticipation. For them, time seemed to have drifted to a halt and in the labyrinth of time all of them seemed to have lost their way. After the news was finally disclosed, all the relatives hid their faces in an attempt to hide their tears.

Before Dr. Zarg made a leave he noticed the old lady, little Ahmed's grandmother, sitting in the corner of the sulked-in room. He went across to her and before he could say anything she began. 'I know you tried,' she gulped, 'but doctor *sahab*, do pray for him, for my little Ahmed *jaan*,' and with these words she lost complete track of her emotions. Dr. Zarg bowed down to kiss her hand and looked straight into her eyes. Her eyes truly did showcase the true pain she felt.

'Your grandson has been like my own child and,' he paused as if searching for words, 'my heart aches just as yours does.'

He gave her a warm handshake and considered leaving immediately. Staying a minute longer would make him feel even more miserable. Tonight he had failed, not in some usual competition or a task but at saving someone's life.

He bade the old lady goodbye and walked his way out of the meshed door onto the pavement that was next to the garden. He noticed Yasmeen who was siting the same way as she had hours ago. While the whole world seemed to have skipped a turn, the spring air did not seem as fresh as it had been hours ago. In the pitch darkness, Yasmeen still sat the same way. The roses in the garden too seemed to have sulked into nothingness as if mourning someone's death. Was she crying or not, Dr. Zarg could not say, but all that he was sure of was that the whole garden seemed to have noticed the loss of a life, a soul that had now occupied the vacant seat of death.

He did not want to disturb her meditation and thus crossed the pathway saying nothing. He turned the knob, again with great effort, and escaped into what we call a normal real life.

. . . .

CHAPTER 2

'You know, she never really liked to stay in the house,' Surbhi began one day while cooking one of Dr. Zarg's favorite dishes. She held the frying pan in her hand and continued, 'also, you know what else I have heard about them?' she said, her eyes narrowing into small slits. 'Yasmeen's mother-in-law would not even let her in the house.'

Dr. Zarg shot a doubtful eye at his wife. He himself had seen and spoken to the old lady and through the little conversation the two had shared he could bet that she was not the kind of lady as being portrayed by his wife. That day Dr. Zarg had noticed something rather mysterious about the old lady's personality. Polite and caring she did seem but her honesty and love for her grandson set her personality apart. She truly was a woman with a purpose in life.

'Poor Yasmeen, first her brother and now…' Surbhi sighed, turning around and at the same time lighting the gas stove.

'Oh yes,' Dr. Zarg sighed, 'Yasmeen must be in a shock.' Yasmeen's brother too had very recently passed away.

Three days had passed since the burial and Dr. Zarg felt it was time he paid his final condolences to the Naqash family. Every now and then little Ahmed *jaan's* demise would make him guilty as if he had committed a crime. For the past week he had not been able to sleep properly and would usually end up staying up all night thinking of Jahangir, thinking of what the poor soul had to face because of someone else's carelessness. Ever since that evening Dr. Zarg's life seemed to have taken a twist instead of a turn and very often he would question his own profession. His guilt, just like the Albatross, sort of hung on his neck flashing its wings all around.

Dr. Zarg always loved spending time in the kitchen, watching his beloved wife cook meals. It was the position of the room that set it apart from the others. The branches of the Chinar tree would dangle against the windows and the sun's rays would often filter through the leaves and illuminate the room like remnants of some faint distant memory. However, today the clouds had conquered the skies and the winds blew every now and then. He could hear his children play in the garden certainly unknown to the fact that one of their friend's would never join them, ever again.

Sitting on the round dining table, Dr. Zarg took out the sketches (he had made on the night of little Ahmed's demise) from his old leather strap bag. He examined the sketches carefully, studying every stroke he had drawn. It was rather queer that he had more confidence in his sketches than he had in his own eyes. He fixed his full moon glasses and drew closer to the sketches when finally he began noticing things he had not seen before. To Dr. Zarg's horror, bruises and cut marks, not of the accident but probably of older incidents, stretched across little Ahmed's slender body. On a closer look Dr. Zarg concluded that the marks were perhaps of someone's fingernails that had been ruthlessly slashed across his innocent body.

All these new inputs called for a deeper investigation. Why was it, Dr. Zarg thought, that little Ahmed had all those bruises and cut marks all over his body? Those marks were certainly not of the accident. Very minor intricate details began hitting him right in his temple and soon everything started to make sense. The knob of that old rusted gate had been too rigid and high for a three year old to have opened it himself. Perhaps someone must have left the gate open. Dr. Zarg snapped his fingers while his breathing sped. All the marks, the gate, all led to one conclusion, someone killed little Ahmed but the question still remained, where was everyone when all this happened. After all, the gate could have just accidentally been left open. Why was little Ahmed, all of a sudden, left unattended?

'She hated her family…. She would always be outside…' Words of his wife, who now was taking some spices out of the cupboard, kept resonating in his ears. Dr. Zarg stared outside the window at one of the lush green Chinar leaves. For people to consider his small hypothesis he needed evidence, evidence to support his accusation, and evidence to prove that a murder had been committed in the household. There were so many possibilities that every suggestion bombarded his brain but something in him, perhaps the flash he had seen, told him that he was heading in the right direction. Without a moments delay he began making his way to the Naqash family.

As he reached the old greasy gate, he checked the knob once again. It was just as rigid as it had been days ago.

'Not in a million years would have a three year old been able to open this rock-hard knob,' he whispered, fixing his glasses. He now felt the need to look around for more clues. Dr. Zarg bent down and began examining the narrow road. He checked the *nali*/gutter that ran right beside the gate and after a much closer look he noticed what seemed to be a very bright yellow ball stuck midway in the gutter. Dr. Zarg pulled his sleeves up and extracted the ball. After much rubbing with a cloth he placed the ball in his bag. There were a series of questions in his mind that urgently had to be answered.

As he crept his way through the gate, to his astonishment he confronted Mary, the housemaid who seemed to have been sitting in the garden. Mary had come to Kashmir from the dilapidated villages of Assam and, to support her family, had started working in Naqash's housefold. Dr. Zarg remembered the last time he had seen Mary, she had been running around little Ahmed in attempt to feed him. Dr. Zarg managed a faint smile even though it was clear that he was taken aback by Mary's presence in the garden. Mary shot up and very politely asked, 'how are you, *Bhaiji?*'

Her voice somehow seemed different this afternoon and there was this shrillness that pinched Dr. Zarg's ears. She seemed to have shed some weight from the last time Dr. Zarg had seen her, so much so that the passing breeze could have now blown her away. Dr. Zarg searched for words and replied, 'Ah Mary,' he fumbled, 'I can't say much about myself, maybe shocked to the very core,' he paused and glanced at the garden. Even though it was the mere beginning of spring, the garden had completely lost its colour.

'...What about you? How do you feel about everything?' He finally completed, now gazing at the flowerbeds. Everything seemed so raw and different than usual and even the flowers had collapsed in their places. It seemed as if all life had literally been vacuumed out of the flowers. Even the buzz of the bees could not be heard in the open air.

Mary narrowed her eyes and in a very husky voice replied, 'Not safe, ever since,' she hesitated, 'that evening, living here seems a.... a nightmare.'

Dr. Zarg's eyebrows shot up and his beard began to itch.

'But. But why, why is that so?' he said rather inquisitively.

'I just don't know sahib, it is the family,' she drew closer and her voice reduced to mere whispers, 'they beat me at times and say that it was my carelessness.'

'And why exactly did they say so?'

'That afternoon little Ahmed was with me but sahib I specifically told Yasmeen *di* to look after him,' she said rather desperately.

'And where was Yasmeen then?'

'In the garden and then she too left for the washroom. Yasmeen di knows it was her mistake and thus she stops spending time in the garden as you can see by the condition. She would spend time here more than she would spend with little…'

'Hey Mary?' Dr. Zarg intruded and from his leather bag he took out the bright yellow ball he had just found in the gutter. 'Do you know anything about this?' Dr. Zarg asked.

Mary's eyes quivered a bit. 'Yes doctor *sahab*, this ball. Yasmeen di had bought it for Ahmed *jaan*, yes, it was this ball but where…?'

Dr. Zarg told her how he had retrieved it from the gutter.

'Mary you wait here as there are some things I need to take care of,' and without any further utterance he strode to the main door.

Over a cup of salt tea, one of Dr. Zarg's favourites, he tried to extract as much as he could from the old lady. Today, however, she looked a lot different than before. Eyes sulked in, lips curled, even her voice was cracking at constant intervals, and from what Dr. Zarg could notice, the old lady had stains of tears on her face.

'His laugh still echoes in my ears,' she said rather mysteriously.

'But Amijan, who left him outside and...' he took out the ball from the pocket, 'why was it outside?'

She glanced at the ball and her eyebrows suddenly shot up.

'Yes, Mary and little Ahmed used to play with the ball,' her eyes sulked again and tears streamed out lining the stained path. So, Mary had played with the ball too, Dr. Zarg thought to himself.

'Oh doctor *sahab*, he wasn't alone, what do I say. It was her, Yasmeen who could not get time from staring at those hideous roses,' she panted. 'She has always been so careless and now see what it has led to,' she stopped, controlling her emotions. She felt she had already let out too much of information and deep down in her heart she felt content, perhaps she needed to let it out, all of her discontent.

Rather confused, Dr. Zarg held the saucer in his hand and sipped his beloved tea from the cup. So, it turned out that the old woman herself felt the same. Her theories are the same as Dr. Zarg's but no, there is one element that still differs. She thinks that it was carelessness where as Dr. Zarg felt it was done on purpose. Someone had deliberately left the gate open. Someone had deliberately played with the yellow ball. Mentally noting all the little data that had been provided, Dr. Zarg now felt it important to speak to Yasmeen in person. Whom does she have to forge the blame on?' he wondered as he helped himself up from the carpeted floor.

'Amijan, I would just want to return the ball to Yasmeen, perhaps she will be looking for it.'

'Ah,' she hesitated. 'She is upstairs but she herself wont know about the ball. It was lost long back.'

Dr. Zarg crossed the corridor and ascended the staircase. He knocked at the door and after a faint response, entered.

Yasmeen was perched on the very same bed where little Ahmed *jaan's* body had been kept the night he had died. She was staring out the window with her chin on her tender hands. Even though the door creaked loudly, Yasmeen did not budge. Outside, the spring clouds blanketed the city stealing away all the daylight.

Dr. Zarg stood near the door for a long while and lost hope for any response. He itched his throat to perhaps distract Yasmeen from her meditation but she simply did not budge. Suddenly, Yasmeen broke the silence.

'You must think I am crazy,' she said, not moving a muscle except for her mouth. Dr. Zarg was taken aback. His throat, which was devoid of moisture, swelled and his eyes twitched.

'No, Yasmeen *jaan*,' Dr. Zarg flustered. He felt his body heat up and he swallowed. It was like a sharp turn in events.

'If you feel I did it on purpose, go ahead.'

'What do you mea..?'

'You know exactly what,' she said, striking her gaze directly at Dr. Zarg who stood with the same vigilance as always.

'Doctor *sahab*,' she narrowed her eyes, 'go tell the world whatever you want to but do remember, I am a woman with a purpose and whatever I do…' she paused and continued, 'I do it for a reason.'

Her words hung in the air, as she looked back outside the window. Dr. Zarg kept trying to make sense of what she really meant. There had to be more, there just had to.

'But Yasmeen ji, I only came here to pay my condolences to your son, for he was just as close to me as my own children are,' he lied, completely forgetting about the ball. His ears now turned crimson. 'Please concentrate on what you are saying as you truly were the only one nearest to Ahmed *jaan*,' he snapped.

Yasmeen chuckled. 'Doctor *sahab*, let's not pretend for the moment.'

'But…'

'Yes doctor *sahab*, I killed my own son,' and with these words only silence followed.

It appeared to him as if the entire world had suddenly come to a halt. No twists, no turns, but a halt. In front of him was a woman who very conveniently accepted murdering her own son. What everyone thought was an act of carelessness suddenly seemed to develop a purpose. Now after the revelation of this small element, the distinction between an accident and a crime was lost.

'I am a woman with a purpose.'

These words struck his ears from all sides. There had to be more to this lopsided plot. How was it that she was dealing with it so casually?

There was nothing more to say, nothing else to do than to stay quiet. In his mind he had reached and played every move up till this point in the scene but what was after this? Awestruck, he simply slipped out of the room.

CHAPTER 3

How was it that the answers to his theories had so easily been dealt with? His throat felt as dry as a summer afternoon in a faraway desert and his hands shivered just like the trailing sand dunes. As he led his way out of the main door he did not once look back. For now his mind had been blocked from all sides and all he did know was that he had to act genuinely and had to concentrate.

The dark grey clouds had finally given in and it had begun raining. Holding his bag tight to his chest, Dr. Zarg crouched and crossed the same old path he had crossed about an hour ago, only now he had lost all incentives to carry on with his minuscule investigation.

'Yes Doctor *Sahab*, I killed my own son.' It was so easy for Yasmeen to say it. Maybe that is why she was least concerned about her son's accident and had spent time in her garden instead.

The more he tried to let go of the words the more they ringed in his head. He was sure that for days to come these words would not fade away into silence and would instead continue resonating in his ears like a rhyme Dr. Zarg had now started to hate. In the labyrinth of judgments and accusations, somehow, his professional self sought the situation differently. His brain wanted to call the police right away but there was something that was keeping him from listening to his brain.

Mary was still out in the garden near the rotten rose beds, the same rose beds that were once stared upon by the killer who was now probably eyeing them from upstairs, humming a triumphant tune.

At the precise moment solitude was the only companion Dr. Zarg could think of that would help him think straight. He glanced at Mary for a second to convey his rush and reached out for the gate when suddenly she spoke.

'What a pity it is that the sight of tonight's moon shall be missed by many.' Her voice sounded heavy and the shrillness seemed to have vanished from her tone. She did not stop. As the rains splashed across her face she continued.

'If it does come out, Doctor *Sahab*, do bathe in the moonlight,' she completed staring at the sky. Her thin neck felt rigid and her gaze had a sparkle Dr. Zarg found unsettling.

'Yes,' he gulped not knowing what to say and added on. 'It does seem that the clouds wont give way that easily tonight,' he finally managed, confused.

'But Mary do take care of yourself and be careful,' and with a final nod he twisted the old rusted knob and left for his room of silence, his study.

With his clothes soaked in rainwater, Dr. Zarg did not consider changing into something dry on reaching home. Instead, he very swiftly made his way to his study, his salvation. He needed this special study of his to think and only think. Yasmeen's words kept on ringing in his ears till he could take it no more. He held his hands tight on his forehead and grunted in frustration. There had to be more to it. Dr. Zarg rewound all the conversations he had during the afternoon and tried to come to conclusions but there was nothing that really convinced him.

Confronting a murder so easily was the easy way out. There is something, he thought, that Yasmeen has not mentioned or maybe she has, just that he might have missed it.

Darkness had now invaded the town and the rains had more or less stopped, however, the clouds still covered every bit of the sky. Suddenly he could see the flash again and this time he swore he managed to peep and see what lay inside it. It certainly was not a play of colours but something with a deeper resemblance to his life. It sure was a flash of realization but realization of what?

Not in a million years had he ever thought he would question a Mother's love for a child, a bond that was once or perhaps still is considered a precious thread that holds the world together.

A tear.

On his study table, Dr. Zarg lay still, chin clasped in his scratched hands, tears trickling down his cheeks. Was it the water from his soaked hair or his tears, one could not say but his face could alone prove to the world that he truly was shattered.

Outside, the winds howled against the window and Dr. Zarg tried to unify him with the wind. It was one of those feelings when he just wanted to fly away. He now tried remembering the flash of light or realization or whatever that it was, but he failed with every attempt.

The flash! He saw it again!

Indeed it flashed yet again and Dr. Zarg leapt out from his chair, jumped to the window and shifted the curtain to one side. He simply stared into the ever-growing darkness. The night had brought with it an uncanny silence that had abandoned the streets outside. It suddenly dawned at him that he had been sitting in complete darkness.

As he struck his sight from one house to the other he only wondered what the families in each of the houses would be doing at the moment. Most of them, he guessed, would be gathered in their living rooms laughing at the much-laughed jokes or perhaps enjoying a quality time with their families. He glanced at the sky and saw the clouds making way for the moon.

'What a pity it is that tonight's moon shall not be sighted by many,' he remembered Mary's words.

What did she really mean when she had said this? He still could picture her hypnotized look, her vicious look when she had said that. Downstairs his wife called him for dinner and just like always he decided to ignore her for the moment.

'So where was I?' he whispered as if speaking to someone in the room. He shot a glance at the bright ball he had placed on the table earlier. 'Mary and little Ahmed used to play with it,' the old lady had said.

'Mary?'

Through his window he glanced from one end to another, trying to peep into the lit windows of the other houses. He was only moments away from turning around when suddenly one of the very bright sources of light went out, and just as it did a whole separate light bulb, in Dr. Zarg's own head, lit for the very first time. The realization!

'The mother had always been in the garden so she possibly could not have been the one who rolled the ball out the gate,' he gasped.

A sudden suspicion drew across his conscience. He narrowed his eyes and tried to look closer at the house that had just lost all it's power and to his amazement he realized that the house was none other's but his own friend Jahangir Naqash's house. In his head he began picturing the way to Jahangir's house and through the window he started counting the number of streets it took to reach there. There was no mistake; it was Jahangir's house that had just lost its power. He checked if it was a power cut but all the other houses seemed lit up, even his own house was well lit. There was only one conclusion. Someone other than Yasmeen was on the go.

'Do bathe in tonight's moon light, Doctor *Sahab*.'

Everything now suddenly started making sense. With his mouth wide open, Dr. Zarg could hardly keep up with new revelations. From his study table, he hurriedly caught hold of a torch, syringe and a phial of anesthesia and rushed his way out of the study room, down the staircase till he reached the main door. Near the door his son's wooden bat rested against the wall. He hesitantly grabbed the neck of the bat, weighed it for a second to confirm his weapon's capabilities and made his way out of the door. Telling his wife about the sudden change in plans would have resulted into a fiasco and thus Dr. Zarg left without a word spoken.

The route to Jahangir's house had somehow seeped into his memory for a lifetime now, thus he reached the main gate in no time. Feeling out of breath, he bent for a while as his lungs felt like exploding. He feared that his chest might burst; nonetheless, considering the delicacy of time, he held out his hand and twisted the doorknob of the gate. No matter how hard he tried, the knob simply did not budge. It had been locked from the inside.

Dr. Zarg looked in both the directions. All street lamps were lit, yet of danger hung in the air. Left with no other choice, climbing the wall seemed the best solution he could think of. He threw the bat across the wall, stuck the torch between his teeth and helped himself climb the wall. After due efforts he climbed up and very carefully set his feet on the other side. The chances of saving a life, yet again, seemed minimal. Tightening the grip around his teeth, he finally jumped on the other side into Jahangir's garden.

Dr. Zarg stumbled a bit but finally held on to his aching feet. Now was the real moment, something he had never done or even thought of doing ever before. In the darkness, only the ruffle of the leaves could be heard, as otherwise all was dead silent. He searched for the bat he had got as a weapon and on finding it, made his way to the main door, which too was locked.

One, two, three and smash! Dr. Zarg kicked his way into the door and broke the murderous silence. Now, at this very instant, the real show had begun. Quivering, he held the unlit torch in his left hand and kept the bat ready in the other. As he walked, the remains of the broken door crumbled under his feet. Sound was the one enemy he wanted to resist at the moment, but alas enemies, just like friends, do not leave your side and stick to you like snails moving across a never-ending pathway. He blinked every now and then and his feet began to shiver unknowingly. As he crossed the corridor and neared the staircase that led to little Ahmed's room, something upfront moved and… smash!

Even before he could sense anything, something as heavy as a log hit him right in the head. He switched the torch on.

A beam of light struck out of the torch and lit almost everything and Dr. Zarg's heart skipped a beat. In front of him, as he had anticipated, was Mary. Her hair stuck out from all sides and her skin was as pale as a rotten orange. Even in the direct beam of the torchlight, her eyes did not quiver. It was not her looks or her eyes that haunted Dr. Zarg but the gun that so very comfortably rested in her confident hands.

Unconsciously, Dr. Zarg's hands slowly rose in the air.

'Mar…Mary?' he hesitated. 'Listen to… Listen to me,' Dr. Zarg's tongue slipped in his mouth and his teeth began to rattle. All his focus directed towards the hole in the barrel. He felt a sudden urge to unravel the secrets that rested within the darkness of that ominous hole. He felt tortured, petrified, stupefied, and all the other words that mean the same.

Mary chuckled, her smile creasing along her face.

'You know doctor *Sahab*, I had a feeling that you would join me sooner or later,' she stared straight ahead.

Dr. Zarg could not keep a track of his words or his memory. All his focus was converged to the very small dark hole of the gun. The flash! His eyes popped open. It was the same flash he had seen on the night of little Ahmed's demise, the same flash he had seen moments ago and now somehow the flash had seeped into the minuscule hole. Dr. Zarg tried concentrating on the immaculate flash of colours. His eyes welled up with tears and soon he could see his son, Habib, and his daughter Shabnam, both gazing in the oblivion.

'These people are not worthy enough to live!' Mary said, her voice rising to a shriek. Dr. Zarg shook his head as if disturbed from a calm meditation.

'You know I used to teach little Ahmed,' she continued shifting to her right. 'I would teach him to follow that obnoxious ball his mother had bought for him and I must say,' her smile returned, 'he was a great learner. He would follow the ball wherever I would throw it,' she laughed, coming closer to Dr. Zarg.

'Why are you even doing this?' Dr. Zarg asked.

'What wrong have they committed that you are trying to kill...'

'Shhh! Doctor *sahab*, at this point in time I would suggest you not to lose your temper,' she chuckled. 'The Naqash family is somewhere upstairs. I locked them while they were busy having dinner,' she said, gazing at the ceiling.

'I don't even know why I am answering you but there are some things you must know before you depart from this world. All of them are beasts and they do not deserve to survive.'

'What?' Dr. Zarg asked in a deliberate attempt to stretch the conversation. He very carefully lifted the bat from the floor and readied the syringe he had filled with anesthesia earlier.

'They ill-treated me!' she shouted. 'I lost my brother because of them!!' Her face got all crimson and her eyes highlighted a diaspora of veins.

In the torchlight, Dr. Zarg could see a tear rolling out of her eyes. As heavy as it did seem, the tear rolled across her cheek down her neck. Her face showed a sudden change in expressions.

'But now, they all must go and die and,' she paused, 'and you should die too.' With a swift movement of her finger, she pressed the trigger and the gunshot pierced through the darkness.

CHAPTER 4

Dr. Zarg was lucky to have noticed the movement in Mary's fingers and just as she pulled the trigger Dr. Zarg slid to the corner.

The torch switched off leaving the place in complete darkness. Dr. Zarg's ears pained due to the loud shot of the gun and it took a while for him to recover to his senses. He could hear Mary approach him and in time he tumbled to retrieve his bat. With a firm grip on the handle of the bat, Dr. Zarg swiped it right through Mary's feet making her crash to the floor. His body now shivered from top to bottom, yet he continued what needed to be done. Mary crawled across the floor but soon Dr. Zarg clasped her leg with his hand. In a split second he took out the syringe from his pocket removing its plastic cover and pierced it in her leg till she could move no more.

Panting, he stumbled back on his feet and struck towards the revolver. He checked the magazine and saw only one bullet missing, probably the only one she had shot. He heaved a sigh of relief and got back to the floor. The others were still safe.

Far in the darkness, the flash reappeared and this time he did not peep inside it, neither did the ominous flash of light reveal its true colours. 'Leaving secrets just as they are works best for me,' he chuckled in his thought. The flash waved in the darkness a little longer than usual but it received no attention whatsoever. It was when it's purpose got lost that the flash lost its way and faded into nothingness.

. . . .

The Chinar trees shone bright under the mesmerizing sun. Out in the garden, where the rose buds were preparing to bloom and the bees were buzzing in the silence, all seemed perfect, yet again.

'But Yasmeen *jaan*...' Dr. Zarg began, gazing at the lush green grass.

'Why exactly did you accept a crime you had never committed?' he asked as his eyebrows shot up.

Yasmeen responded instantly. 'Doctor *sahab*, my Ahmed *jaan* was the sole purpose for whom I lived and now that he had been snatched away from me, there was nothing really left of me,' she said. In the bright sunlight, her eyes sparkled giving out a peculiar touch of magic. For a change she felt different, or perhaps better.

'Doctor *sahab*?'

'Hmm,' he responded.

'This garden was just as close to me as was my little Ahmed and that was exactly why I would spend so much time here outside,' she smiled. 'In the roses I could see little Ahmed smiling at me and it was this love that kept my gardens in such a pleasant shape. 'But,' she paused, her eyes sensing some terror, 'on the eclipse of my Ahmed's demise, as his life was being taken away from him, my roses too sensed his absence,' she glanced at the rose bed. 'Soon, the roses too stopped responding and before anyone even knew, I got to know it first that my *jaan* was no more.' A tear trickled down her cheeks and got wiped across her face by the passing wind.

'Dr. Zarg. I am sorry if I made everything hard for you,' she said apologetically.

'No. No. Not at all. Perhaps it was this habit of yours and of course your sudden confrontation of the crime that made me realize that it was not you,' he swallowed. 'Otherwise I would never have had looked out of my window,' he said. 'I understand your reasons and you did the best as a mother.'

'So Mary has been taken away?' Yasmeen asked.

'Yes, after the police came that night she was immediately taken to the hospital. She has been diagnosed with schizophrenia. All of it was a big delusion. She imagined everything, from being tortured to having had her brother killed. In fact she never had a brother. So, in short it was a sort of delusion of persecution that had led her to attack all of you. I wish we had known, for we could have saved a life.' Dr. Zarg said apologetically.

The rest of the conversation ran into the details of Mary's awkward behaviors. As for Dr. Zarg, time in the garden simply flied. As he spent all of his free time, it was now time for him to return to those rotten prescriptions.

'And yes, Yasmeen *jaan*, before I bid adieu, how is Jahangir doing?' Dr. Zarg asked with utter concern.

'He is doing very well, although everything has left him traumatized and he still has nightmares, but all the more better than before. He recently joined his office work too,' she answered confidently.

'And Ami *jaan*?'

'She is fine, but still at times shouts at me for staying here, out in the garden for so long,' she said, blushing.

As Dr. Zarg made his way out through the same old rusted gate his heart felt content. He had been successful with his very first crime investigation, which gave him a hot topic to brag about for days to come.

The End

A DUSTY ROAD TO HEAVEN

Is there a heart in the desert's eye?
Where shadows play with the only light.
Have you ever dreamt of the starry night?
Where all you can see is life's only plight.

There once was a time when life went by,
Like a stream through a corpsed forest.
But, now that I look at the same very spot,
Only a dream in its place flows.

It is not water that runs through its course,
Neither are there any unearthly creatures.
Rather, there is a thought, pure and untouched,
That smoothens every rock and pebble in its way.

Very soon the dream too runs away,
And all the world's forests' do collide.
Soon the starry night turns shadow black,
And leaves me aghast for the night.

Dust settled, the night rustled, and only
A few could be seen.
The trees smashed and down it came,
The road to Mighty Heaven.

It did not end there, Oh! How could it end like this?
For fires lined up throughout the path.
My legs shuddered till they could move no more,
My soul shivered till it could live no more.

I was floating, not in the air, but,
Across the dreamy path, I flowed.
I lived even without living, yes,
I dreamed for once and for all.

Butterflies, Bats may not reach me
As I soar into this lust-less bliss.
The sun's rays may not reach me,
But I shall finally rise and shine.

It had to end, oh yes, it did.
As tears filled the imageless rivers.
Hope, Love, was all that echoed
Throughout this dusty road to Heaven.

The Marlet's Curse

For Burhan Bhai and Shayan,
I have no words

CHAPTER 1

No sound could be heard. Everything, it seemed, had come to a halt in this long forgotten corner of Marland. No birds chirped here, no grasshoppers played and no poppies grew in this ruin.

The Divine Lake, which was once the main attraction of Marland, lay devoid of any life. But, what was so divine about this barren lake, one may ask. In the olden times the Lake would bloom with flowers every spring and the birds would live in harmony here. There was this unfathomable power that resided in the lake until a day came when everything changed... forever. There was a time when, through widespread channels of rivers and streams, the water from the Divine Lake would reach every corner of Marland. No tree would be left untouched by the lake's seraphic powers and now, a time had come when no tree is spared from the deathly curses the lake is used to spread.

Something moved on a tree nearby and out from the darkness emerged an exceptionally large bird. As it soared into the skies, its wings sliced the damp air. Soon the figure began circling the lake as if a night's guard. Blexter's carefree wings flapped with immense strength and even though it was nighttime the pitch darkness did not pose any problem to his flight. Very soon three more figures, just as large, formed a sort of procession and whirled around the Divine Lake.

These were the Marlet Kites!! It's their curse!! Again!!

In the star-less sky, the four kites circled the lake non-stop. Was it their ultimatum strength or a natural cause, one could not say, but the winds began to blow with tremendous strength now, shaking the trees to and fro.

'*Doroso*,' Blexter blurted in a hurry. 'I want you to take *Afifa* and *Jinx* to the other end of the lake.' *Afifa* and *Jinx* were Blexter's sisters and *Doroso* his younger brother. Blexter's voice was somewhat hoarse and his beak rather pointy. A red mark, that did not seem to have faded in all the years that had passed, stretched across his right eye. While his feathers were a mix of black and brown, his head was awfully white.

Doroso adhered to his elder brothers commands and spread his left wing wide. As Afifa and Jinx slowed down, Doroso flew to the other end of the lake. In the meantime, Blexter reached the center of the lake and in an instant, with one strong flap of his wings, saw his muscular body spiral into the delicate skies. Blexter stuck his wings against his body and just like a lightening bolt, he flashed into the skies.

Everything looked different from this height. Blexter could very well notice the disastrous effect of the curse they had been performing over the years.

He looked up and shut his eyes in prayer.

'O'Marlow, O'Marla, O'Marlet
Sting the very bee that fought or fret
Let the divinity show its divine powers
Help us spread this curse across the forest!'

At this point all the clouds of Marland raced towards the Divine Waters. Within seconds the whole lake was covered in thick fog and clouds. Thunder rattled from all ends but Blexter did not stop. He maintained his position through periodic flaps of his wings and continued. A smirk now stretched across his face. With his head held high and eyes still shut, he embraced the crackling sound of the thunder.

'Give birth to the curse on his eighth birthday
Till then he shall rest but,
A time shall come when he bows before every second
And never shall fly through that holy line'

From below, the four kites too bolted their way into the skies, spiraling into the darkness.

'Well, it is true that one man's prayer can be other man's curse,' interrupted Afifa, giggling. Her voice carried a sudden shrillness that pinched Doroso's ears and in return he stared at her, a signal for her to shut her trap.

Mid-air, the four Marlet Kites maintained their flaps to stay put, a skill they had mastered quiet well.

All four very distinctly remembered their flight lessons as young birds with their father. Every now and then they would recall the torture they had faced due to him. They remembered how he would attach heavy stones to their claws and would order them to fly long distances till their claws would scale and bruise. 'It takes a lifetime to be a worthy Marlet Kite!' Their father would shout at them.

Just as all four of them completed their prayer, Jinx broke the silence. 'We now have to throw the ingredients of the curse into the lake,' she shouted on top of her voice. The purple winged maw-hawk that crowned her head waved in the blowing winds.

'Blexter!' Jinx called out, looking directly at him. 'You release your *feather* and Doroso,' she paused shifting her gaze at him, 'you throw one of your *toe nails* this time, but make sure it's pointy,' she completed, pressing on the last words. 'Afifa will use her *tear-drop* to warm up our ingredients and I have already readied the *tail* of the chameleon,' she said over the howling winds.

'Okay, on the count of buggs,' Jinx shouted while the others readied their ingredients. 'Let's show that obnoxious plum-headed parakeet what happens when one deceives a Marlet Kite. 'Ready? Sticks! Stones! Buggs!' and in an instant they opened their claws. The four ingredients, very silently, made their way through the thunderous clouds and dropped safely into the Divine Lake. Just as the ingredients fell into the water the four Kites shouted in unison.

'Fly through that holy line!'

Despite the loud thunder, their voices echoed in all corners of the lake. The curse had not yet been set. The four kites glided their way to the surface of the lake and continued circling its circumference, only now with immense speed. Very slowly the still water of the lake began to swirl. The winds too began to blow with immense speed snapping the trees out of their roots and a whirlpool now appeared at the center of the lake.

Smirks flashed across the four Marlet Kites' faces and they now began to slow down. The curse had now been set!!!

'Doroso?' Blexter began in his same commanding voice. 'Kill that plum-headed parakeet and his wife but,' he paused, 'but, let their child survive. He is going to live a hell of a life.' Blexter completed while Afifa and Jinx giggled. With a swift nod, Doroso flapped his way out of the Divine Lake to complete the task that had been set forth by his elder brother.

In the heart of the Divine Lake a red light flashed and it grew brighter till everything got still, yet again. The clouds retrieved, the winds stopped blowing and the darkness settled too.

CHAPTER 2

8 Years Later

Her jet-black feathers complemented the night and her tears swept across her face as she bolted across the starry sky. The crisp moonlight could reveal only a tiny portion of her dull face. Her grey beak, which was perhaps the only part of her body that was not black, twitched continuously. Even though it was a night full of bright stars, no star reflected in Hebetha's sulked eyes. Her floppy flight made it difficult for her to focus at her destination.

As Hebetha neared Wiselton, all her thoughts got clustered into a heap of confusion. She began her search for the Red Pulped Firetree but unfortunately lost her way. Wiselton sure was the most complicated town in the whole of Marland. With probably a variety of thousands of trees that shot into the skies, the town lacked any symmetrical pattern.

Hebetha's heartbeat sped faster in desperation. This wasn't the first time she had lost her way to the tree. She shot her sight from one end to the other when finally she could see an extremely bright source of light flicker in the distance. As she neared it she heaved a sigh of relief. It was the Red Pulped Firetree she had been looking for.

The outer surface of the tree was filled with Pulped Poppins that shone bright under the moonlight. Hebetha had always been fascinated by the power of the Poppins as a baby-crow. It was just a little unfortunate that tonight her curiosity did not lie in the flowers she so admired. It was something else that had snatched her attention; something she had prayed to the Gods never to happen but her prayers had gone unanswered.

Hebetha traversed within the tree and soon spotted the thick branch beside which lay Mr. Greywill's Tree-hollow. As she landed over the branch she realized how she had never visited this Red Pulped Firetree post midnight. What could it have been that had made Hebetha fly to this corner of the forest at such an odd time? What indeed?

Habetha opened her beak to speak when suddenly a raspy voice from within the tree spoke.

'You do believe me now?' the voice asked casually. Hebetha lay shocked, her eyes terror struck.

'How did you…' she whispered, moving her feet closer to the hollow when suddenly she remembered how she had been instructed never to peep inside it.

'Shh, child, lower your voice,' Mr. Greywill interrupted, 'the snakes and the other spies are all around,' he warned. No one had ever seen Mr. Greywill or even dared peep inside his Hollow. He too had never set a foot outside it.

'Mr. Greywill, it is true,' Hebetha blurted in desperation. 'All that you had said has come true,' she sobbed. A faint wind blew across her face making a few Poppins dance.

'Of course child, all of it is true. Why would you then expect an old bird, as old as me, up all night? Dear Hebetha,' he sighed, 'I have been waiting for this night for quiet a long time now,' he paused, waiting for Hebetha to answer.

'The signs, Mr. Greywill, Buck is showing the signs of the curse,' she said abruptly. Buck was Hebetha's adopted son. She had adopted him when Buck had only been in his egg.

'Hebetha, I know and thus I had warned you earlier, but…' his voice trembled.

'…but only I did not listen,' Hebetha completed the sentence, her face terror-struck. 'It is today, his birthday,' she paused, 'and my boy will be plummeted to death,' she cried.

'Shhh. Hebetha, the snakes are on the watch,' he reminded her. 'Hebetha, I know a way that will help your boy survive,' his voice drew into a deep thought, 'but for that I need to see him. Bring the boy to me, to this hollow. The time is right, my child. Believe in your step-son and he will believe in himself.'

'Hebetha,' Mr. Greywill continued, 'your son is the only one who can break the curse. Get the boy to me and I will help him. That is all that I can do for you dear child.'

Hebetha's eyes quivered as she fixed her eyes at the darkness inside the hollow.

'You must let him go, Hebetha, for his own good and for that,' he paused, taking in a deep breath, 'for that you might have to be a little harsh.' With these words the truth stabbed Hebetha's heart drawing a deeper wound than before. She had never let Buck out of her sight, except for the times he would go to his school, and now she was to leave him alone in the forest? Impossible!

She let out a deep sigh. There was no other choice. Without another word she descended into the wild darkness.

Mr. Greywill too let out a very deep concerned sigh. As he saw Hebetha's minuscule image far in the horizon, the thought of Buck's eggshell he had preserved all these years, struck his mind.

'Reddnut,' he called out. Sounds of someone's swift movements could be heard from the branches above. The ruffle of the leaves grew louder when out from nowhere a young **squirrel** landed onto the same branch where Hebetha had sat minutes ago. His tiny paws had mastered the art of climbing trees and his royal brown fur helped him camouflage when needed.

'Reddnut, go get Buck's eggshell,' Mr. Greywill whispered and without a nod or any sort of response, Reddnut left.

'The time has finally come,' Mr. Greywill thought to himself. This was the only chance there was left to bring justice across Marland.

⊶⊷

While the moon continued showering its cold light in the starry skies, still no winds blew. Hebetha's joints and her wings had never felt so tired. With every flap of her wings a feather or two struck out causing a surge of pain across her body, but at the moment all of this was least of her concerns.

She ran the conversation she would have with Buck, her stepson, in her mind again and again but nothing felt convincing. As she neared Shadowshade, the land of the darkest and the wisest crows, she grew even more restless.

The large Banyan trees covered most of the land in Shadowshade and the Pebblefall streams made this place the ideal location for the survival of the crows. They are lazy, you see.

As Hebetha searched for her home, long forgotten memories (for no particular reason) began playing before her eyes. She could see Buck's egg in her hand, as clear as ever. She could feel that glitch her insides had felt when she had held the egg for the very first time. The vibrant colours of shell, its shine and its scratch-less beauty had made her gasp in amazement. Suddenly a surge of terror and hatred ran within her veins as now her husband, Draven, appeared in her memories banishing the egg and snatching it from her until finally it fell from her wings.

'No!!!!' Habetha screeched while her tail fluttered. It was only old memories, she realized, and tried to calm herself.

She quickly located her home in the darkness and landed on one of the branches at the very top. Her body showcased a terrible loss of feathers and her job here had only begun. Very carefully she made her way to the heart of the tree where Buck's nest rested. A steady breeze shook a few leaves off of the tree and a few clouds could be seen floating in the distance.

Hebetha wasn't surprised to notice Buck's nest empty. Buck had always been excited about his birthdays; she remembered how his eyes would shine the brightest on this day. Hebetha looked around when her eyes finally fell on Buck's tiny silhouette on a branch that stuck out of the thick canopy of leaves.

Under the crisp moonlight Buck's colorful body shone bright and one could notice the wide combination of colours that very elegantly coated his body. His bobble head was mostly red while his beak was a dark shade of maroon. The most awe-inspiring feature of this young plum headed parakeet's body was not his long tail but a black neck collar that very elegantly separated the colours of his head from the rest of his body. His long red-tinted wings enhanced his beauty and would leave his cousin crows flabbergasted. This morning, however, there was a slight variation in his body. The tips of each of his wings had turned cold white and his tail had curled at the very tip.

It seemed as if the moon's alluring beauty had hypnotized Buck. Hebetha too, for a moment, stared into the magic of the moonlight. She strongly desired to vanish inside the moon's mighty force, away from all her misery, but soon she too snapped out of its hypnotic powers.

As she glided towards the branch, where Buck was sitting, she doubted if her heart would be able to reveal the harsh reality to him and confront its consequences.

'Buck?!' she broke the silence as she landed over the branch. Buck's body gave a sudden jerk and his eyes came back to life. He turned towards Hebetha.

'Oh, mother, I didn't realize...'

'Buck, we don't have much time for this...' Hebetha snapped. 'Buck,' she swallowed, her heart pounding against her delicate chest, 'you are going to come of age and I feel ashamed to say this but you have feasted over our food for too long now,' she said abruptly as her heart shackled into countless pieces.

'Ma, What...?' Buck asked puzzled.

'You must go. You have to leave and you must do it now. Draven was right, we should have never adopted you,' Hebetha trembled.

'Buck take what you feel is important but leave. You can't stay here any longer. I was laughed at by the others for raising you up but now you are a grown up bird and you can take care of yourself,' Hebetha cried.

'Ma, are you al…' Buck uttered, moving a step closer to Hebetha.

'Leave, leave before the others wake up,' she paused, tears pouring out of her eyes. 'They wont know the difference.'

A strange silence settled over the tree.

'But, where am I to go?' Buck asked, desperately.

'Go to Wiselton. I have booked a Tree Hollow for you there,' she lied. 'Search for Mr. Greywill, he is the owner of the Hollow. Think about what you would want to do for a living and then work on your own,' she looked away trying to hide her face. Hebetha was a poor liar and perhaps had never really lied, but today it was important.

Buck flustered as his insides screeched from within. 'O… Okay,' he fumbled.

'I understand what you are trying to say ma…' he paused.

'Thank you for all your love and warmth,' Buck said as his eyes welled up with tears too. For him it seemed as if the entire world had suddenly spun the wrong direction. With a swift jerk of his wings he took off and continued flying without a glance backward. As for Hebetha, she cried uncontrollably, mourning the departure oh her beloved son, well, stepson. The moonlight suddenly seemed to have lost all beauty, and the stars, well it felt as if they never really existed.

. . . .

CHAPTER 3

Reddnut very easily made his way down the rough surface of the tree. His association with Mr. Greywill dated back to a time when the vicious Marlet Kites had been powerless and were yet to rise to power. It had been unfortunate that the very soul who had let out the age-old secret of the curse was the very first one to be cursed. He very vividly remembered the night Mr. Greywill had revealed the secret of the curse to the kites. What a disastrous night it had been!

His muscular tale waved as Reddnut galloped through a heap of leaves. He slowed down, took a sniff of the dry air and continued prancing along the long grass till he reached a bare field. In the open sky a few clouds now blocked the moonlight making it difficult for Reddnut to see anything in his way. He stood on his scrawny limbs, scratched his nose and continued his search until finally he smelled what he was looking for. Without any further delay, he began digging. As he dug the hole he recalled the day when he had buried Buck's shell at the very same spot, he remembered how horrifying the weather had been that awful night.

'Reddnut, keep this shell safe, safer than anything you possess,' he could hear Mr. Greywill's terrified voice again. He remembered how scared Mr. Greywill had been that night.

Soon all the voices in his head vanished. He realized he had dug enough. Inside the pit was an eggshell that was broken into two halves. It felt only yesterday that Reddnut had hid the eggshell under this barren ground. He cupped the two shells, one within the other, tied it around his back and began his return.

'Thank you Reddnut,' Mr. Greywill began as Reddnut untied his string and placed the shells aside. 'Did you lookout for the Spyrous Snakes?' he asked nervously.

Reddnut responded with a firm nod. He had always been a very quite creature.

'I wonder what is taking the parakeet so lo…'

From within his hollow, Mr. Greywill could see a tiny figure approach the tree. Reddnut rolled the shells towards the hollow and pushed them inside. His job here was done.

He waited for a command but on hearing none he simply spiraled along the bark of the tree and disappeared.

Mr. Greywill waited patiently until finally the figure landed on the branch next to his Hollow.

'Ex… Excuse,' Buck panted, shattering the silence.

'Do not come closer Buck, dear child.' Mr. Greywill interrupted.

'But how,,,?' he sounded confused.

He gathered his courage and very boldly asked, 'are you Mr. Greywill of Wiselton?' his voice trembled. 'My mom has booked a hollow,' he said devoid of any confidence. In his head, Buck pictured vicious snakes rattling out of the hollow. He took a step backward and waited for a response. In the distant horizon, the red tinge of sunrise could now be seen.

'You have nothing to fear child. Yes, I am Mr. Greywill, but my introduction is not important,' Mr. Greywill began softly. 'Buck, I wish I could explain everything but now is not the time,' he completed.

'What do you mean?'

'Buck, as every second ticks, you are losing the little time that is left in your hands,' Mr. Greywill began.

'Buck, there is a reason why you were raised amongst crows. There is a reason why the tips of your wings are turning white,' he paused. 'Buck, the Marlet Kites had cursed you when you were still growing in your shell.'

Mr. Greywill's soft voice stung Buck's ears. Why in the whole world would the Marlet Kites waste a curse, that too on Buck? All of it seemed a joke, as if a prank his mother was playing on his birthday.

'Your out of your mind!' Buck exclaimed, tightening his claws around the branch.

'Buck, I know that you dream of a waterfall every night and I also know that you drown in it. Buck I have dreamt the same dreams, but right now I cannot tell you much,' he said as his voice reduced to mere whispers. Buck's heart plummeted to the very bottom of his chest.

'How did you…?'

'However Buck, I have something that will help you,' he intruded. From within the hollow Mr. Greywill pushed the eggshells out. The eggshells rolled till they reached Buck's feet. Buck held out his wings and grabbed it. Although the shell seemed muddy, which suggested that it had been buried, its vibrant colours were still visible. His eyes fell on some words that had been inscribed along the surface of the two halves of the shell.

'Is this the shell I was conceived in?'

'Yes Buck, this is your shell. Buck, you were the only bird in the whole of Marland who got cursed while still in an egg. If you see those inscriptions, well, those are the verses of the curse the Marlet Kites used on you,' Mr. Greywill paused, 'Buck, the reason I saved this shell all these years was because all the curses that the Marlet Kites use have a hidden solution. Since I am cursed myself I cannot tell you where to go, for that shall put both of us in danger but...'

It was evident that Buck was confused and so Mr. Greywill tried his best to explain things properly. '...but your solution to all your questions lies in those inscriptions. Buck, searching for your answers will be hard but you will have to exceed all your limits to fight the curse,' he paused as if recollecting some thoughts. 'There is a reason we dream of a waterfall, there is a reason why both of us drown in it every night. All your answers lie beyond the Bolster mountains.' Mr. Greywill hinted.

Buck glanced at the inscriptions one more time. Waterfall? Bolster Mountains? Nothing that Mr. Greywill said made any sense to Buck.

'Buck?' Mr. Greywill whispered, 'child, break the curse, break that vicious curse forever!' he said in agony.

'The curse will only take a day to spread, before it will kill you,' Mr. Greywill warned.

Buck shut his eyes. Far in the east the sun rose out of the horizon, coloring the sky in a shade of orange. Where was he to go? What was he to do now? Everything seemed a mess. Memorizing the little hints Mr. Greywill provided, Buck prepared his flight. Just as he prepared to take off, Mr. Greywill's voice reached out to his ears.

'Now Buck, before you go, I must remind you to **stay away from your loved ones**, for you are just as dangerous a threat to them as they are to you. The curse gets stronger when you are with someone you love. It feasts on care and compassion,' he completed.

Bearing Mr. Greywill's last words in mind, Buck took off.

'All the very best, son,' Mr. Greywill whispered under his breath knowing that the branch lay empty.

. . . .

CHAPTER 4

'Sire, I have received all the reports from the Spyrous Snakes,' Aganta said panting. Being a purple sunbird, Aganta had been rather extraordinary at spying and would always manage to get fresh news for her masters. In her career as a spy her small size had never created a problem for her, instead, it had made her swift, jubilant and a very sturdy servant. Her beak was a mix of black and grey and on her neck was a dark blue spot that helped the Marlet Kite's distinguish her from the other purple sunbird.

'And what do you have for us?' asked Blexter who seemed least interested in the conversation. He sat on a relatively narrow branch in comparison to his large size. As he spoke his eyes lay fixated at his reflection in the steamy lake below. In the horrific years that had passed, the Divine Lake had changed miserably. What once had homed thousands of birds and fish had now turned into a massive cauldron that the kites used to spread their curse. It was said that both 'prayers' and 'curses' had been discovered here in this part of the Forest.

Steam rose from every corner of the lake. There once was a time when every living bird would pray and rejoice the presence of the Lake but now no one ever came near this dilapidated dump.

'Sire, it's Mr. Greywill,' said Aganta in panic. The blue spot on her neck sparkled in the presence of the fuming steam. 'The snakes say that the old scum-corn has hinted about the Divine Lake. Mr. Greywill has helped someone seek the answers to your curse,' she completed.

'And with whom,' Blexter paused. He looked away from his reflection and stared deep into Aganta's eyes. 'With whom did this old friend of ours share the knowledge of the curse? I mean no one can break the curse without knowing the verses, besides Mr. Greywill is already cursed and if he tells anyone he will die that very instant,' Blexter said, swinging one of his foot from the branch.

A chill ran down Aganta's body as Blexter's eyes shot directly at hers. 'He was…' she hesitated. '…Mr. Greywill was speaking to one of your…' she fumbled and in the same breath continued, '…one of your cursed victims. I…' she sighed, '…I, I have his name too.' she finally blurted, expecting some praise for her dedicated work.

'It is a plum-headed parakeet, Sire,' she said, her eyes giving out a peculiar sparkle, 'and… and his name is Buck, they say he turns eight today, sire, and… and,' she sounded impatient, 'and his curse spreads today!' she said in excitement. There was a moment's silence but suddenly Aganta remembered another very important information she had missed out on.

'But, sire,' she said hesitantly, 'Mr. Greywill gave Buck the egg-shell he was conceived in and… and the verses of the curse have been inscribed on it.' She completed fearing that something bad was to follow.

'Hmm… now that does ring a bell,' Blexter said casually as he rose to his feet.

'Aganta, how long have you been working for me, for us?' Blexter asked. He took a Chime Bone (a large bulb headed bone of a Dancing Jackal) and began banging it against the bark. Terrified, Aganta took a step back.

'Si… Sire,' she hesitated, 'it's been eight years,' she shouted over the loud thuds of the bark.

'Oooh, well, now everything rings a bell,' Blexter said giving a hysteric laugh. Soon the thuds grew louder echoing across the Divine Lake. Aganta looked from one end to the other. Just as she took another step back she realized that she had reached the very end of the branch. She looked back, only to find her steamy, terrified reflection looking back at her.

As she turned back to face Blexter, her heart nearly skipped a beat. In front of her stood not one but all four Marlet Kites, gawking at her.

'Doroso,' Blexter began, breaking the horrific silence. 'Aganta here has a message for us,' he chuckled, 'and she says that our dearest Mr. Greywill has hinted about the Divin…'

'But shouldn't he have died,' interrupted Jinx. 'I mean didn't our curse restrict him from revealing the secret of the Divine Lake? He would die, he should…'

'I said hinted,' Blexter snapped, losing his patience. 'The curse we had used on him never restricted him from helping the others. That owl is wise and knows how to twist things. We have a bigger problem at hand. To break our curse one must have the knowledge of the verse and unfortunately,' Blexter paused, 'well, unfortunately one of the creatures we had cursed years ago has those verses and Mr. Greywill helped him.'

'Aganta,' he continued now staring directly at her. 'Do you kno…' he cleared his throat '…do you know who used to work for us before you came along? Do you know anything about your predecessor?'

Aganta had not known anything about her predecessor. Was there even one, she thought. Perplexed, Aganta chose to stay silent.

Blexter looked back at the others in search for a response.

'Mr. Plum-headed Parakeet!!' exclaimed Afifa. 'We had cursed his son!'

'Yes Afifa, that son of the Parakeet is going to join us soon.

'Do you remember the curse we had set on him?' asked Doroso who had not spoken in a very long time. His voice seemed dry and all the more hoarse.

'It doesn't matter. There is only one revelation to all the curses. There is only one place in the whole of Marland from where one can break the curse, remember?' answered Blexter. 'Mr. Greywill was cursed never to speak of that place but having had the verses of our curse he must have easily helped out that Parakeet,' he said.

'Si... Sire,' Aganta hesitated. 'Is he a threat, sire? I can kill him if...' she paused, watching Blexter approach him. Aganta's heartbeat lost rhythm and her legs shivered uncontrollably. She shut her eyes in despair.

'Aganta,' Blexter whispered, 'we really want to trust you with this news but if by any chance this spreads, the whole of Marland would go against us. You see, all of them would hope for our loss and you know the power of hope,' he smirked.

His voice up so close ran a chill down Aganta's spine. 'You have been a faithful servant,' and with a swift swipe of his sharp wings, Aganta's body swept off the branch and spiraled down into the steaming lake.

Blexter neared the very tip of the branch and watched Aganta's body dissolve in the acidic water.

'War is not war without killing a few acquaintances,' he whispered as he walked towards the other Kites.

Even though Buck had barely begun his journey towards the Bolster Mountains, his body ached miserably. His wings felt a little heavier than before while his insides literally burned. He felt the need to check on his wings and just as he did his heart sunk. Large portions of his wings had turned cold white and it was evident that the curse would spread faster.

There certainly was no time to lose. To reach his destination faster Buck first had to know the destination. Where was he to go? What was the significance of the waterfall he dreamed of? 'All the answers lie in the verses inscribed on the shell,' Buck remembered Mr. Greywill instruct him. He knew that there was more relevance to the inscriptions; only he had not given it a thought.

'No wonder Mr. Grey… or whatever that his name was, asked me to take it along,' Buck thought to himself.

Hailing from a safe environment, adventures like these had always been a distant dream for Buck. Up ahead he could see a cluster of very dark clouds approaching him. He stiffened his tail and tightened his grip around the eggshell in preparation. Just as he neared the thick layer of clouds, something out from nowhere flew towards him and hit him hard on his right wing. The collision shook Buck from head to tail. He tried to search for the attacker when his eyes fell on someone he had known since childhood.

It was Ella, his childhood friend who studied with him in the Parakeet school. Her right eye twitched continuously while her grey-patched head shook in excitement.

Buck could see that Ella was trying to signal something. She chirped as loud as she could but her voice was barely audible in the midst of the loud thunder.

Ella had always been a dear friend of Buck's, and was perhaps his only childhood friend. Buck spot a large Gulmohar tree down below and motioned Ella to follow him. Very swiftly the two birds glided through the mist and landed on a thick branch that was covered with lush green leaves. The tree was gigantic in comparison to the other trees around and was covered by a sheet of miraculous red blossoming flowers. The clouds covered most of the skies, completely blocking he sunlight.

Just as the two birds landed, Buck hastily slid the eggshell aside, gathered a short breath and began.

'What are you doing here?' he asked in excitement. Buck was unable to express himself properly.

'Are you an idiot?' blasted Ella. She could not fix her eyes on anything but Buck's white-patched wings. While growing up, all the teachers in the school had always appreciated Ella's chirps but today her voice sounded too shrill. 'You fool! Who flies straight into a dark cloud?'

'Wha.. What are…?'

'That is not the question Buck,' Ella gasped for breath. 'You must never even go near a cloud that dark... Didn't you learn anything in the school? We learnt it all together!' she shrieked.

'Ella but how did...?'

'I,' she cleared her throat and very uncomfortably said, 'Buck, I have been following you.'

'Following me?' Buck repeated.

'Yes, Buck I have been following you. In the morning, right before dawn, I saw you pass Puddletown and well, I have been following you since,' she confessed.

'But why? How could...'

'See, I told you. That is not the point Buck,' she gasped for breath. 'Buck, you are following the wrong direction. You won't reach the Divine Lake flying south. You have to fly southwest to avoid the Katilik Range and follow the direction till you see the opening of the **Bolster Mountains**. Understood?'

Buck hesitated to say another word. 'How did you know I was heading towards the Bolster Mountains? Have you been eavesdropping on me?' Buck asked furiously. 'Leave this once Ella and don't return.'

'And let you die?' she replied. 'Buck, you have to face it. You need me and I know I can help you. Buck, you could have died in the lightening! Buck, you can't do this alone. I heard what Mr. Greywill told you an...'

'But I will have to do it alone Ella,' Buck shouted. 'It is not a game, it is a curse for Great Willows sake!' His eyes were close to popping out.

'Ella,' Buck said, trying to cool down, 'you have to leave me.'

'And I choose not to. Buck, your body is already,' she paused and looked at his frail wings, 'your body is already so weak, you wont last long if left alone. I can help you reach Bolster Mountains and I am willing to do so,' she said, gasping for air. Nearby the lightening continued and it began to drizzle.

'Buck, there is a reason Mr. Greywill gave you that shell this morning. Just look at it,' she said as she pointed towards it. 'He must have preserved it all these years for a reason.'

'Ella I'm terrified,' Buck spoke silently. 'I don.. I dont kn..'

'Shh... Buck, I can understand and I strongly feel that your shell contains all the answers you are looking for. Didn't you hear Mr. Greywill? Your answer lies somewhere beyond the Bolster Mountains.'

Buck's eyes widened in realization. He grabbed the eggshell in haste.

'Ella, let's search for the answers!' Buck exclaimed. He brushed the surface of the shell with his wings and began reading out the curse.

'O'Marlo, O'Marla, O'Marlet,' Buck read. Soon Ella too joined him and began reading the inscription aloud.

'Sting the very bee that fought or fret,

Let the divinity show it's divine powers

Help us spread this curse across the forest'

Having read the first half of the curse, Buck took the other half of the shell and continued reading.

'Give birth to the ...' Ella narrowed her eyes in attempt to read. 'Give birth to the curse on his eighth birthday,' she managed.

'Till then he shall rest but, A time shall come when he bows before every second, And...' both of them hesitated. 'And never shall fly through that holy line' they completed in unison.

'Buck,' Ella whispered shortly after narrating the curse, 'I think I may know where to go.'

Buck's face lit with a smile. He could finally see a ray of hope.

. . . .

CHAPTER 5

'Buck,' Ella continued thoughtfully, 'the first stanza of the curse is rather misleading, or,' she snatched the shell from Buck's wings and read the curse again.

'Sting the very bee that fought or fret!' she repeated as if trying to make sense of the words.

'The answer to this curse is here some…'

'But Ella I don't have time for this!' Buck interrupted. 'All I was told was to fly towards the Bolster Mountains. Ella,' he paused, swallowing dry air, 'I have to reach there as fast as I can or… or I will die.'

'Buck, where will you go after reaching the Bolster Mountains?' Ella interrogated. 'This curse points to one place where your destiny lies and that is precisely why I am searching for all of the clues…'

'I understand Ella,' Buck said. 'But,'

'I might know what this curse means, just give me another moment,' Ella said.

'Let the divinity show it's divine powers,' she read and suddenly realized something rather intriguing.

'Buck,' she looked at him straight in the eye, 'most of the verses tell us how and when the curse will spread however,' she paused, 'there is this one line which is thought provoking,' she held the shell high and pointed at the very last line of the curse.

'And never shall fly through that holy line,' she read out in excitement. 'I know what this means Buck, well, I think I know.'

'And that would be?' Buck asked in anticipation, losing his patience.

'Don't you remember what Mr. Jolly Windmate taught us in the chirping lessons?' Ella asked. As for Buck, he could not recall any lessons with Mr. Jolly Windmate. Buck could only gather some faint memories of Mr. Windmate's long boring lectures and his exceptionally long red beak. Noticing the blank expression on Buck's face, Ella understood that she would have to elaborate.

'Well,' Ella said, rolling her eyes. 'Buck, he once taught us about the Divine Waters, how due to the deteriorating quality of the air around the area the songs of a Parakeet now sound different than before, he…' she paused expecting Buck to complete the sentence.

'Ah, don't you remember?' she asked in frustration. 'He once taught us about the waterfalls!' Ella exclaimed in excitement.

'Buck, the Divine Lake channels out into four waterfalls and these waterfalls then form various tributaries. Thus, the water from the lake reaches the whole forest!'

'That could be right,' Buck said thoughtfully. 'I dream of waterfalls!'

He remembered how Ella had always been interested in geography lessons and all the topics related to the waterfalls.

'Also Buck, Mr. Windmate told us about this one special waterfall, you must remember that?' she asked. Buck did not respond and only waited for Ella to speak more.

'Well, there is this one waterfall that is surrounded by the Holy Trees and these trees absorb the curse from the water and make the water pure! It is the Wondrous Falls, that's where you have to go. Buck, this makes the Wondrous Falls the?' she asked finally expecting an answer.

'The holy line!' Buck completed. 'I have to fly into it!'

'Exactly!' Ella exclaimed

Buck's insides felt totally different now and he was more enthusiastic to fight for his life. He knew where to go and what to do. Half of his problem was solved.

'Ella, you must stay here. It might be dangerous,' Buck said earnestly.

Ella shot a red eye at him. 'Buck if we are going, we will go there together.' she said very crisply.

Buck fell silent. A passing poppy smothered across his face and he only stared at it, wondering where it must have come from.

Ella's back shivered in pain and her wings began to ache. It had nearly been seven hours since Ella and Buck had begun their journey. The Bolster Mountains seemed close yet they were still quiet far away.

Buck, on the other hand, did not show any exhaustion. Even though his eyesight had weakened and could barely see the horizon, he was still determined to fly to the world's end if it came to that. In the hours that had passed, his body had shown absurd transformations. All that was left of his colorful body was a faint shade of green and a completely dried face. His face did not reflect dreams any more. He longed for the return of the beautiful colours that had once adorned his body.

It was close to sunset and the sky had already gotten dressed into a shade of orange. The sun set the whole forest ablaze with it's divine light. As Buck stared at the hazy sunset, a horrifying thought struck his conscience. This could be the 'last sunset' of his life. It was only a pity that his eyes were not capable enough to capture it all.

As he bid his last good bye to his old companion, Buck concentrated on the wide Bolster range that awaited him. He caught a glimpse of Ella every now and checked if she was all right. It made him miserable to watch Ella undergo all the pain for him, for the sake of his survival.

As both of them saw the North Star, which shone bright in the twilit sky, all of their excitement subsided. Buck was closer to his unknown destiny and scared even more. From above, The North Star stared at both of them with utter distaste, shedding its cold light on them. The day had finally come to an end and a very dark night awaited both of them.

'Almost there,' Ella whispered to herself as both of them continued their journey. Down below, the barren stretch of land gave way to a rather rugged terrain. This marked the beginning of the Bolster Range. As they glided over the mountains they could notice the rocky terrain filled with nothing but trees.

'Turn left,' Ella shouted, sounding slightly exhausted. She raised her right wing and stiffened her tail to glide leftward. Ella glanced from one end to the other in her search for the Divine Lake.

The mountains rose high making it difficult to glide freely. Ella began losing her patience. She desired to rest but just as her body was about to give in, she saw the Divine Lake shimmer in the distance. Her eyes lit up.

'There!' Ella shouted in exhilaration. 'We have reached the Divine Lake!' she shrieked.

Ella's shriek shook Buck who had, yet again, taken refuge in his long forgotten memories. He saw Ella pointing towards the space between two gigantic mountains ahead, beyond which the lake shone in innocence. The mere sight of the lake cured Buck's pain. Both Ella and Buck held their breaths tight and glided towards the lake. As they reached closer the condition of the lake shocked both of them. In school they had been taught about the immaculate beauty of the Divine Lake but all those dreamy descriptions were a complete contrast to what they saw in front of them.

Poisonous steam exuded from the hot surface of the lake. All the trees around were uprooted and had collapsed one on top of the other. The air too was foul and for some reason both Ella and Buck felt very unsafe.

As they reached the center of the lake both of them halted in mid air.

'Which way do the Wondrous Falls flow? Buck asked.

'Well, it should be far in the east near that narrow opening,' Ella began, pointing at the nearest mountain that walled the lake. 'You see that opening?' she asked. 'Well, that is where the waterfall lies, but Buck,' she paused, struggling to hover in mid air, 'we have to go around that wall of mountains and not straight ahead. If we go straight we will be right above the waterfall and the force of the air will pull our bodies down along with it so, it would be safe if we simply go around the mountain. It should take about an hour more to reach there, Buck!' she shouted in excitement.

'So, we will... Ahhhh!' Ella screamed as something banged into her. The force with which the creature hit her shook Buck. Buck tried to maintain his balance but his wings could not bare the force. It was only after due efforts that he could fly properly. He twisted three sixty in search for Ella and saw her struggling to recover. Ella flew next to Buck and both of them began searching for the attacker. In the distance Buck saw a gigantic figure dash towards them.

As the moonlight revealed bits of the figure, Buck could feel his heart go still. Ella too turned in Buck's direction and lay motionless.

One of the Marlet Kites was flying towards them while both of them lay star struck. Far beyond the skies, Buck could feel the North Star smirk at them.

. . . .

CHAPTER 6

'Fly!' Ella screamed and both of them bolted in the opposite direction.

Ella's face had turned grey. The heavy fog made it difficult for them to fly. Buck tried searching for the kite but he could see nothing. No one followed them, not the kite, not even their own shadows. Just as he twisted his head he banged into something. He agitated to control his balance but just as he opened his eyes, he felt like dropping dead. He was in for a surprise!

This time not one but two broad vicious kites stared at them. The kites truly were as swift as the night. As the kites continued staring at them, Buck could see both had a smirk across their faces.

One of the two kites tried to slice Ella into two halves. Ella was lucky enough to have dodged the attack tactfully. She held on to Buck's wing and gave him a nudge as both of them bolted. The two kites were on the periphery of killing them. Ella began her search for a hideout. She spot a random tree on the lakeside and flew towards it. No sooner had she landed that she noticed Buck missing.

She shot her sight in all possible directions but in the thick fog she saw no sign of Buck. The darkness obscured her vision too. She could hear a flutter of wings nearby. She craved to call out for Buck, to let him know where she was, but taking any risk would put her life under threat. Had the Marlet Kites caught Buck? Far in the distance she could see the blurred shadow of one of the Marlet kites.

Something moved on a branch overhead and her heart sunk into the lowest compartment of her chest. Through the untidy branches she could see the tiny deformed figure approach her.

'Oh, Buck!' she sighed in relief.

'Shhh!' Buck signaled. 'They are all around us.'

Buck was as pale as the winter's moon and struggled to stand on his feet. All the energy that was left in his tender body seemed to have completely run out. He rested one of his wings against the bark of the tree and shut his eyes in despair. Every inch of his body pained and there was nothing he could do about it.

Buck searched for a tree hollow and luckily found one. He mildly poked Ella and signaled her to follow him into the hollow. The tree hollow was completely empty. The stench within it was unbearable but it served as an ideal place to take refuge.

'Buck, what do we do?' Ella whispered. 'We are losing time.' Her voice was hoarse and it was evident that she had not had pure water in a long time.

Ella noticed some rotten hay beneath her feet. It was a pity that a place such as this was no more anyone's home. She gazed at Buck's moonlit face and her heart skipped a beat.

She could see Buck's enigmatic colours ruthlessly being snatched from his body. The pain felt so real to her. Buck rubbed his beak and lay shocked at the sight of his wings. Every feather on his body had turned white and seemed so heavy that it was a miracle that Buck had not collapsed on the hay as yet.

'You've grown so weak,' Ella whispered softly. Her eyes watered as words flowed out of her beak, 'and you said you would do this alone…'

In the deathly silence she gazed at the sky and could still see the dark silhouette of the Marlet Kites gliding over their conquered skies.

Ella noticed Buck's beak move and she got closer to hear him. It took great efforts for Buck to force words out of his mouth

'Eh… El,' he muttered. 'Ella, help…. help me get up,' he said.

She had to bear the pain of watching Buck's white body suffer. She held Buck up and waited till he could balance on his feet.

'I still have some st…' Buck hesitated as his head.

'I still have some strength,' he said frailly. 'We have to search for the Wondrous Falls before dawn.'

'Buck, I have know exactly where to go and how we must go about it. Do you see that mountain ahead,' she asked, pointing at the two mountains that shared the same origin. 'You see the narrow opening between the two, well that is where the lake gives way to the wondrous falls,' she said.

'But Buck, there is a change in plan. Instead of both of us going in the same direction, we will split ways. I will go first. Even if the kites follow me, you will go around the mountain, into the waterfall,' she hesitated, 'and you will break the curse.'

'What?'

'Buck, I will divert their attention while you must lead your way into the falls, I …. I know it is a little time consuming but it is the only way, okay, so please cooperate,' she said.

'But, that is dangerous, no, no, I won't let you risk your life,' Buck revolted. His voice had found the perfect tone of resentment; only Ella was not ready to buy a word.

'Buck stop!' Ella cut him short. 'This is our only chance! I am waiting for the kites to rest and we will make our moves once they are out of sight. You are going to have to follow my rules!' she commanded, panting.

A strange silence filled the hollow while the two stared into each other's eyes. Ella checked the sky again and pressed her eyes for a better view. To her amazement she saw the skies clear. Her morale boosted two fold. Wasting one more second would have severe repercussions and thus she readied her flight.

She poked Buck and signaled him to prepare himself for yet another tiring journey. Ella hopped on to the edge of the hollow and waited. She was not sure if now was the time to make a move. She heaved a deep sigh and instantaneously bolted out of the hollow. Buck too hopped on to the edge of the hollow and soon after Ella had taken off, he let himself free and flew into the skies.

His wings reflected all the moonlight that fell on them. No matter how much he tried to pay attention at his flight, he wound up staring at his wings. 'It will all end soon, for the better,' he consoled himself. He followed Ella's plan religiously and flew towards the mountains. Even though it took longer than he had anticipated, he enjoyed what could be his last moments alive. Having crossed the mountain, he now flew towards the Wondrous Falls.

From this other side of the mountain, the lake was barely visible. A loud shriek pierced Buck's ear and he halted mid air. His spine went cold and his wings almost froze when another loud shriek could be heard. The shriek butchered the innocent silence. Was that Ella? Had they killed her already?

In the turbulent air, he found it hard to flap his wings. Even though the sound of the waterfall could be heard, Buck chose to search for Ella instead. Suddenly his eyes fell on four gigantic figures coming straight after him.

'It was now or never.'

A voice ringed in his head as he saw the Marlet Kites, all four of them, bolt towards him. Their vicious faces were ignited with hatred and vengeance. Buck mustered all his strength and followed the faint sound of the waterfall. He continued flying without a look back.

Here on the other side of the mountain, all seemed different. With no sight of the Divine Lake, this area was rather dry with hardly any forest cover. As Buck flew he only concentrated on the faint sound of the falls. The gush of water grew louder as he dwelled deeper into the forest when he could finally see the Wondrous Falls through his own eyes. The moonlight made the Wondrous Falls shimmer in the darkness.

Buck could see Ella near the Wondrous Falls waiting for him. Far in the horizon the sun was about to come out and mark the beginning of a new day.

Slowly everything got silent and instead a very soft voice resonated in Buck's ears. 'This is the most delicate time dear, treasure it,' the voice said. Buck remembered his mother, Hebetha, narrating stories about the magic of sunrise. He had been so safe with her, so very comfortable around her. He desired to hear her voice again but no voice followed. Instantaneously, the gush of the Falls returned and with it returned the sound of misery and pain. In the midst of all the noise he could hear Ella's voice calling out to him.

'Buck! Hurry up!' he heard Ella shout. 'They are right behind you!' Just as the words escaped Ella's mouth, Buck turned his head and to his horror, he saw the four kites only miles away from him.

Buck readied himself for what could be his last flight. He stuck his wings close to his chest and held his tail up high. He forged all the strength that was left in his ghostly body and with a loud bang bulleted towards the Wondrous Falls.

Far in the east, as the sun reached the very locus of its origin, Ella could see the sky take the color of blood.

'Buck, hurry up!' Ella cried on top of her voice.

The Wondrous Falls was all that Buck could see now. He devoted all his energy to reach the spectacular waterfall. Who was he doing this for? Who was he saving himself for? Was he doing this for his stepmother who had loved him with all of her heart, or his family, or his friends or was it…. or was it…?

He charged towards Ella, who had gotten wet under the splashes of the falls. Ella held out her wing and Buck clasped it with a strong grip.

… or was it Ella, for whom he wished to continue living, who gave him an incentive to live and whom he now lov…

Just as the sun gave birth to the young golden morning light, Buck, with his wing clasped tightly with Ella's, flew directly into the Wondrous Falls. The robust flow of the water pushed Buck down but posed no problem to him. Buck managed to flap his wings every now and then and succeeded at staying put in the water.

The four Marlet Kites watched Buck's body twirl in the most graceful manner possible. All four of them did nothing but stare at Buck's elating body. All the light from the sun converged to the spot where Buck flew and all of his colours slowly returned.

With his head held high, Buck now struggled to move his wings. Just as the warmth of the morning sunshine reached his inner soul, he snapped his wings wide open. All the sunlight now reflected off of his crystal feathers and struck directly at the four Marlet Kites. Their feathers began to shed and their beaks burnt down to ash. Afifa collapsed first, and soon the other three followed. The water of the Wondrous Falls invited the defeat of the Marlet Kites.

The Marlet's curse had finally been broken!

. . . .

CHAPTER 7

His wings did not hurt anymore and he felt all of his energy, his strengths return. For a moment Buck could feel his body devoid of any pain or misery. Was it rebirth or did he really succeed at breaking the curse?

Buck rejoiced watching his colours return, however, his happiness was reduced to half when he noticed someone missing, someone who should have been present there celebrating with him, but simply wasn't. Ella could not be seen anywhere around. All the warmth left his body as he forced his way out of the waterfall in search of Ella. He looked in all the possible directions but failed to find her.

For Buck, the sun's raise lost all its power. Even the gush of the water did not reach his ears. He dashed to the bottom of the waterfall and continued his search. Moments later he noticed a small figure quivering on a rock near the Wondrous Falls. On closer speculation, Buck noticed that the birds' wings had been robbed of all the feathers it earlier had and its tail seemed to have broken. Ella was struggling to survive.

Ella's neck shivered rigorously while her body juddered uncontrollably. As Buck held her in his wings his body too went cold. His eyes welled up with tears. Cupped warmly in his wings was someone whom he utterly loved, yet he could do nothing to save her. He tried to press her chest but only water came out of her mouth.

'Stay away from your loved ones, for you are just as dangerous a threat to them as they are to you.' Mr. Greywill's voice resonated in his ears. The water of the Wondrous Falls may have been a cure for Buck but for Ella it was acid.

'Ella,' Buck whispered. His voice trembled as words escaped his mouth.

'Ella,' he repeated, desperate for a response. Buck's eyes felt as if on fire till a tear trickled down to extinguish the pain. Buck shut his eyes in silence when suddenly he could hear the faintest of a whisper. Unimaginable! Buck could hear a voice reach out to him. It was Ella's voice for sure but he failed to comprehend as to what it was trying to say. He hugged Ella's body tight and concentrated on the voice that had no source.

'In Dreams, do believe,' the voice said. Buck held his head closer to Ella's body and could finally hear her properly. The source of this 'voice' wasn't her mouth but her delicate heart.

'In yourself, do believe.' Soon Ella's voice faded and gave way to the noise of the surrounding.

'Ella!' he shouted as tears streamed out of his eyes.

Ella sighed one last breath as her eyes stared deep into Buck's. Deep inside, Buck's heart shattered into pieces.

No words escaped his mouth or hers and all the sounds and sensations of this world, for Buck, lost meaning.

The sky was clear and soundless. The occasional breeze reassured Buck of the world's existence. The Divine Lake lay still and for a change reflected the bright sunshine that fell on it. Things were so different now, so much better, ever since the Marlet's Curse had been broken

On the thousands of rejuvenated trees rested birds who had come from different parts of Marland. These were birds of high stature and of poor background alike and had summoned to the Lake for a reason.

An owl stood on the very edge of the lake and beside it stood Buck. Both Buck and the owl held on to a *Boliminous* leaf that very carelessly floated in the water. The leaf was decorated with what seemed to be Marland's most exotic and beautiful flowers and within it lay a bird's corpse.

Buck's face lacked all emotions, and as for his wings, they lacked the mere strength of completing this last task set forth for him. This last task was to set the *Boliminous* leaf free.

'Dear Buck,' Mr. Greywill uttered, breaking the monotonous silence. 'Are we ready?' he asked

Buck's eyes quivered as he heard Mr. Greywill speak. He gathered his thoughts, thoughts that had mastered the art of running away without being expressed, and finally answered.

'Yes.'

Hebetha, who too was present there, flew towards Buck and hugged him tight.

Buck let out a deep sigh. He stared at the soil for a while and just as he looked up, he gave a final push to the leaf. Soon Mr. Greywill began his prayers.

'The world's shall shower peace and joy,
While the sun will listen, quiet at rest.
Her soul will shine bright and will,
Rejuvenate this, our Divine forest.'

Mr. Greywill's voice resonated across the forest. As he completed his prayer, the thousands of birds that had gathered all around shouted with joy.

'Rejuvenate this, Our Divine Forest,' they chanted.

With loud chirps and roars, the birds flew in the sky, free and fearless. A new era had begun.

Buck's eyes followed the trail of the *Boliminous* leaf. Just as it reached the very center of the lake, the ends of the leaf magically covered Ella's body and soon sunk in the lake. His beak flushed red and a smile emerged within the ends of his beak.

'Rejuvenate this, our Divine Forest,' he repeated.

What Ella had given him was more precious than life itself. She had gifted him a meaning to his life and he treasured it more than anything in this world. As all the birds chanted the prayer back to their homes they wondered how the curse had actually been broken.

Buck closed his eyes and stood still. In his head only the thought of the leaf in the far oblivion, existed still.

The End

ACKNOWLEDGEMENTS

I remember going through some novels in my school library when I came across this very brilliant line in one of the books, which read, 'No man is an island.' And I choose to begin with the same words.

'No Man is an Island' – John Donne

Truly, this collection of stories and poems could not have been possible without the immense efforts of all the teachers I have had since childhood. Every teacher, be it from Tyndale Biscoe School or from Welham Boys', has contributed in someway or the other and I am grateful to each one them.

I would like to express my gratitude to the English department of Welham Boys' School especially Ms. Rushmee Rawat, Ms. Joyeeta Mukherjee, Ms. Indira Mahajan, Ms. Monica Chandel, Ms. Deepali Singh and Mr. Saurav Sinha, who guided me in every which way and taught me how to edit my own works. I would also like to thank Mr. R. Srikant who never hesitated to counsel me and taught me lessons beyond the reach of textbooks. My teachers have played an immense role in shaping me as a human being and the bond I have created with each one of them is simply inseparable. I would not have given voice to my thoughts had Ma'am Bindra, Headmistress of Welham Boys' School, not encouraged me to continue with my book when I myself was doubtful of the idea. She would always be eager to know about my progress and it was precisely her enthusiasm that gave me the strength to write.

My family has played a major role in all of my endeavors. To know that your presence matters and that you are being supported no matter what makes you stronger. It would take a whole new book to thank all of my uncles and aunts for their love and care. When I was unable to find an editor and decided to edit my work on my own, it was my cousins who helped me restructure my stories. Mir Hubiba, Sheikh Dania, Ayat Muneer Shayir, Khudaija Riyaz and Mehreen Khan were one of my first readers who helped me understand the 'reader's point of view'. I am grateful to each one of them.

When I initially joined Welham Boys' School, I feared that I would not be able to adjust. Now that four years have already passed, I cannot thank God enough for the opportunity I was given. Welham taught me how to be independent, how to live life to the fullest but most importantly, Welham gave me friends with whom I share memories I shall cherish for the rest of my life. I can never repay Devyansh Rai, Pranav Gupta, Prithvi Agrawal, Amol Agarwal, Aastitva

Jain, Nikhil Kumar, Ashish Vardhan, Junaid Jan, Yash Goel, Harshun Mehta, Tenzing Namgayal, Umair Wani, Parth Babbar, Sagar Singh, and all my other batch mates who always supported me with my writing. They were always so eager to know about my book and always gave me accurate remarks about my works. A special thanks to Mahika Jha who helped me believe in myself and made me realize my true potential. I would not have managed to finish my stories without her support. I am ever grateful to Siddhant Gupta, Vainee Bhatyal, Gauri Sinha, and Shreya Sharma, who always supported me through e- mails and always managed to cheer me up.

Everything about this book was a true struggle and I get goose bumps thinking about how it all had started. I realize now how much I learnt from each and every struggle I faced. Just like any other writer's tale, looking for a publisher was a challenge. I was a student at a boarding school with minimal connections and in no way could search for a publisher. I thank Farrina Gailey and Mary Oxley, whom I have never met and have had conversations only through mail and phone, for pushing me beyond my limits and helping me meet my deadlines. I wish both of them best of luck for their future endeavors.

Last but certainly not the least, I would like to thank my parents for their constant love and their faith in me. They gifted me with the best childhood one could ever have and with that an amazing life. I could not have come this far without my Dad's endless support. He always encouraged me with whatever I did and gave me enough space to take my own decisions. My mom, on the other hand is the one person whom I cannot thank enough. She is the mother and a guardian everyone deserves. My mother was my tutor, my friend, and also the best storyteller one could ever get.

Sheik Safwan Fayaz

ABOUT THE AUTHOR

Sheik Safwan Fayaz is a grade XII student at Welham Boys' School. He received his upper primary education from the C.M.S. Tyndale Biscoe School and D.P.S Srinagar.

Safwan was the chief-editor of the school magazine at Welham Boys' School, and gained major writing experience working in the editorial team. He aspires to study International Relations after graduating from school.

While growing up Safwan took keen interest in fantasy fiction and imagined a world of his own which he then named Ghardavia. Through this collection of stories and poems Safwan wishes to bring his childhood imaginary world back to life. One of his stories, The Enchanted Phirran, is set against the backdrop of the 2014 floods.

Safwan can be reached at safwanfayaz123@gmail.com

Printed in the United States
By Bookmasters